PASSIO

When her job in Vancouver collapsed,
Natalie fled to the refuge of her father's
ranch in British Columbia—to find her
father had just died and the hostile Cal
Hendricks was in charge. And her old love
Murray Elson was now married to her best
friend. Where did Natalie go from here?

Books you will enjoy
by ELIZABETH GRAHAM

MADRONA ISLAND

Seven years ago Kelsey Roberts had destroyed Lee's life, and she had hated him ever since. Now they had met again, and all she could think of was at last getting her revenge. But how was she going to exact revenge from a man who didn't even remember her existence?

KING OF COPPER CANYON

Because she considered she and her mother were fully entitled to some of her grandfather's estate, Dani had gone up to British Columbia to confront Grant King. But instead she found herself holed up in a cabin miles from anywhere with a disreputable character named Burt. How could she get away from him and start sorting out her personal problems?

DANGEROUS TIDE

Toni had put all memories of her unhappy marriage to Jay Stanford behind her and was now thoroughly enjoying her job on board a cruise ship to Mexico. The last person she had expected to meet there was her ex-husband—accompanied, needless to say, by Gloria Powell, who had been the cause of the divorce. But Jay, it appeared, had expected to meet Toni . . .

JACINTHA POINT

To save her father from rotting in a Mexican jail, Laurel had been forced to marry the masterful Diego Ramirez, a man she did not know and certainly did not love—how could she, when she was happily engaged to Brent? And then Diego made it clear that the marriage was not going to be in name only . . .

PASSIONATE IMPOSTOR

BY

ELIZABETH GRAHAM

MILLS & BOON LIMITED
15–16 BROOK'S MEWS
LONDON W1A 1DR

First published 1981
Australian copyright 1981
Philippine copyright 1982
This edition 1982

© Elizabeth Graham 1981

ISBN 0 263 73703 9

Set in Monophoto Baskerville 11 on 12 pt.

Made and printed in Great Britain by
Richard Clay (The Chaucer Press) Ltd,
Bungay, Suffolk

CHAPTER ONE

CARL BERMAN glared across the desk, the vein at his temple distending as he met the stormy gaze of the girl seated opposite. Angry, she was like a roused tigress—a beautiful tigress, with her tawny hair and gold-brown eyes, dangerous like any ruffled feline. He sighed and said resignedly,

'It's just not working, is it, Natalie? When I promoted you to be my assistant, I'd thought that——'

'I know damn well what you thought!' she interrupted abrasively, delicately chiselled nostrils flaring her contempt. 'You don't fool me, Carl, you're as sexist as any of the account executives you thought I'd land for you! "Let's see what you're like between the sheets before I commit myself to the paper kind," ' she quoted mockingly between lips shaped by the gods for just such a pastime. Soft, full, warm with honeyed promise; even the venom in her words lost their sting when they emerged from such sweetly contoured enticements. Carl Berman sighed again.

Had his motives in hiring her as his assistant in the advertising agency he had built up himself been entirely free of the taint she accused him of? Maybe not. Competition was fierce in the business, and a pretty face certainly couldn't do any harm if it influenced clients in his direction. Even he, in his early forties and happily married to Bernice, his wife of twenty years, couldn't have refused easily when confronted with a girl like Natalie Forman.

'Whatever the reason,' he acknowledged tacitly, 'it's just not working, is it?'

Scorn twisted the full bow of her mouth into a grimace of anger. 'Did you expect it to, in those conditions?' she flared, the soft wool of her gold suit jacket falling intimately into place over the firm high thrust of her breasts as she leapt to her feet and eyed Carl with flaring indignation. 'Do you know what it feels like to be used as you've used me, Carl? To be picked up and thrown on the heap when you don't deliver what's expected?'

'Now, Natalie,' he soothed, rising himself and going round the desk to place a placating hand on her suited shoulder, 'I'm not throwing you on the heap. I'll see that you get something else, something more——' he hesitated delicately, 'more suited to your talents.'

Natalie shrugged off the paternal hand. 'Don't bother, Carl,' she chipped icily as she moved in jerky motions to the door, 'I have plenty of opportunities open to me.'

Plenty . . . the word echoed hollowly in her head as she descended by elevator from the tenth floor occupied by Berman Associates to the ground floor which gave on to the bustling downtown centre of Vancouver. Early tourists to Canada's Pacific Coast city mingled with the regular hustle of mid-afternoon shoppers and a traffic flow that would increase tenfold when offices and stores closed at the end of the commercial day.

The delicatessens lining Robson Street held no

urgent appeal for her at that moment. Normally she would have stopped to look, savour mentally, then buy for that night's dinner. But these weren't normal times. The knowledge that she was jobless pounded into her head with each step she took on her way to the apartment she had rented three years before on coming to the sea-girt city on the coast. At a premium now, the apartment she had rented at a reasonable price overlooked the Lost Lagoon at the entrance to Stanley Park, the thousand acres of rural beauty set at the heart of Canada's most prominent Western city. Swans nested there in spring, proudly displaying their offspring as they paraded them across roads oblivious to the traffic that assaulted on either side. Black squirrels, darting and curious, deserted the green stretches of the park to climb telephone poles and wires and gaze bemusedly at the occupants of structures far more confining than their own habitat.

Uncaring now of the animals whose lives she shared on a limited basis, Natalie let herself into the apartment, shucking off the confinement of her jacket and tossing it on the bed in the room to her right before entering the living room with its windows overlooking the serenity of the Lagoon. She had no eyes for the comfortable red plush of the overstuffed sofa and flanking armchairs, the contrasting stone colour of the broadloom carpet that swept from wall to wall. In the compact kitchen adjoining the dining area she ran water into the electric kettle and plugged it into a wall socket.

Low-key fury outlined her trimly contoured figure as she dropped into one of the four round-backed dining chairs and stared unseeingly through the window straight ahead.

Plenty of opportunities, she reminded herself sourly. The only problem was that most of those opportunities involved shorthand and typing and all the assets of a trained secretary ... which she was, basically. She had worked in just such a position with Berman Associates until Carl had taken a flying leap on her abilities in other directions.

She caught the soft line of her underlip between her teeth as she rose and attended to the boiling kettle, absently spooning instant coffee into a grey stoneware mug and carrying it back to the round dining table.

Who else would give her a chance to spread her wings, to fly in the world of business, as Carl had? Her aspirations in the field of advancement to better things had been destroyed that afternoon in Carl's office. She was a whiz at secretarial work, but a lot less desirable as an executive, however junior her position.

But how could she go back to the nine-to-five routine, typing the letters she herself had dictated for the past year? The humiliation to her spirit would be too much, too deep to bear. What she really needed was a break from the hustle-bustle of commercial life, a time to lick the wounds Carl had just inflicted upon her. Fleetingly, a letter she had received from her father a month or so ago impinged on her consciousness. He was ill, he had written, but she wasn't to worry. He had taken on a capable man who would take care of the ranch until he himself was well enough to resume the reins.

What better place to hide away than a ranch in the beautiful interior country of British Columbia? Already she could scent the new growth of May, the dull thud of horses' hooves on the range made moist by the spring run-off from far-sited hills. She could recover there, re-establish her priorities in the familiar landscape of her childhood.

Besides, it was time she went to visit her father. She hadn't been back since before her mother's death two years before. Battling with 'flu at the time Joanna Forman had died as quietly as she had lived, Natalie had made no appearance at the funeral. Doug, her father, had understood . . . as he had always understood the only child of his union with Joanna.

An upwelling of choked affection made Natalie firm in her quickly formed resolve to go home . . . home to be with the father who had adored his wife and idolised his daughter.

Her eyes still held the brightness of tears when she got up to answer the insistent ring of the desk phone in the living room.

The last rise over the hills surrounding Doug Forman's property was as comfortingly familiar to Natalie as was the outline of her slim fingers on the wheel. She changed gears to mount the slope that would give her a view of the entire valley where her father's brown and white Hereford cattle would be grazing contentedly on the lush grass emerging from pastures too long covered by crusted snow. Feed would have been distributed during the long cold months of winter, but nothing tasted like the fresh growth of spring.

To her either, Natalie reflected wryly as she directed her small blue and white sports model down the accompanying grade that led indirectly to the house where she had been born. Bridget would be there with her strong lilting Irish voice, to welcome her.

'Come on in now, me darlin',' she would say, her plump cheeks wreathed in smiles. 'I've a stew simmering on the stove that will make your stomach glad to be alive!'

How could she have left the home, the people she loved, for so long? Because her mother was no longer there to preside over the smooth running of the big ranch-house? That must be it, because it was impossible to think of Blue Lake Ranch without the gentle presence of her mother forming a quiet background to the Formans' home life. A lump rose and refused to dissolve in her throat. Joanna Forman had been the salt of the earth, the quiet spinner of gentle webs which enfolded everyone in her environment. She had been a good neighbour, a staunch friend in time of need, a devoted wife and mother. The kind of woman Natalie could never aspire to be.

Her foot lifted from the accelerator as the house came into view at the end of a long sandy driveway bordered by full-growth jackpines. Low-roofed and sprawling, the house spread before her in the mellowed half-light of a late spring afternoon. From one of the barns across the stockyard, a solitary figure detached itself, the white blur of face reaching curiously in her direction. Not her father. Someone different.

The forest green legs of the suede pants-suit she was wearing swung out from the car and her feet touched the fine silty sand of the parking area in front of the house. The man, whoever he was, must be one of the newer hands, perhaps the one her father had mentioned in his last letter. Dismissing him from her mind, she left her luggage in the car and went to the arched wood door leading into the main part of the house. The door was, as usual, unlocked.

'Dad? Bridget?' she called lightly as she stepped into the familiar sight and odour of the entrance hall, the polish Bridget used rising pungently to her nostrils. 'Anybody home?'

There was no response, and Natalie's senses were assaulted by the unused air about the place. It was as if she had stepped into the familiar confines of a recurring dream, a dream where everything was as it should be yet not as it should be. Had her father mentioned in the letters she skimmed over briefly that Bridget was no longer with him? A cold clutch at her heart sent her feet scurrying towards the rear kitchen, relief flooding through her when she saw Bridget's comfortably padded form bent over the huge white stove in the far corner.

'Bridget?'

The woman started and turned, her face paling as she looked at Natalie as if she saw a ghost from the past.

'Natalie? Is it really you, child?'

'I called, but you didn't hear me.' Affection welled in her for the woman who had shared the mother role in her life, and Natalie ran across the stretch of red tiles to throw herself into the arms that had soothed her childish cuts and fears. It wasn't until she moved back and looked at Bridget with tear-studded eyes that she noted the defeated look in her eyes, a strange suggestion of gauntness in the fleshy cheeks. A childish tremor of fear went through her. Bridget was never ill, never altered from the comfortable anchor she had always been.

Quelling the fear by pushing it to the far recesses of her mind, she forced her voice to brightness. 'Where's Dad? I wanted to surprise him, but I guess he'll see the car outside.' The car he had presented to her on her eighteenth birthday, the car he and her mother had gazed forlornly after when it bore their only child away to a life that was strange to them.

Bridget seemed to choke as she turned away from the bright enquiry in Natalie's eyes. 'If only you'd come sooner, child,' she got out, her workworn hands clutching the raised side lip of the stove she had laboured over for years.

'What do you mean?' An even colder fear clutched deep in Natalie's innards. Had something happened to her father? An accident on one of the tractors, a traitorous kick from one of the horses that were his pride and joy? 'Has something happened to Daddy?'

'What Bridget's trying to tell you,' a harsh voice interjected from the doorway behind her, 'is that your father——'

'No! Not like that, Cal, have some pity on the child,' Bridget swung round to glare fiercely at the newcomer. Natalie had also faced about, wondering if the man's appearance would match the hard cold-

ness in his voice. It did, but she had no time then to
appraise more than just a few of the hardbitten features
before the gravelled tones came at her again.

'A person who gives no pity deserves none herself.
Why should she be treated with kid gloves?' Hooded
brown eyes shifted from Bridget to Natalie, and she
flinched at their open contempt. 'Your father died
last Friday,' he said bluntly. 'He was buried yesterday.'

'*No!*' Natalie whirled on Bridget, seeing the truth
of the man's statement in the emotion that clouded
the older woman's normally sparkling dark eyes. In
a whisper she went on, 'It's not true, it can't be true.
Why didn't you tell me? I'd have come, you know I
would have come.' Her fingers groped for the hard
wood of a kitchen chair pushed under the centre
table, and she sank into it frozenly.

'Like you came when he wrote to tell you he was
ill?' the harsh voice ground into her whirling senses.

'I—he didn't seem to be—that ill,' Natalie
choked, not questioning for the moment the
stranger's right to accuse her as she sought for remembrance of her father's scrawled words.

'Of course he didn't,' Bridget stepped in to defend,
moving at last to come and place a comforting arm
round Natalie's stiff shoulders. 'You know Doug
didn't want her to know, bring her from her job in
the city.'

'How could you not let me know that he—he'd
died?' Natalie cried wildly, addressing the question
to Bridget although it was the man called Cal who
answered.

'How could we let you know?' he rasped with an

anger that strangely seemed to arise from a deep pain inside him. 'You were taking a long weekend off from your goddamn job and you couldn't be reached at your apartment.'

Natalie stared numbly at the expensive leather casual shoes that matched her pants-suit. It was true. She hadn't been at the office because she had lost her job on Friday, walked out of the building and gone home. Home to the sudden bleakness of her apartment, making up her mind to come back here to lick her wounds.

But there had been that telephone call from Brad Evans of Evans Chemicals, and a last-ditch effort to redeem herself in Carl Berman's eyes.

She hadn't been able to go through with it. Even landing a plum of an account like the Evans one had weighed low in the scales against her knowledge of what she was doing. Was keeping her job worth the loss of her self-respect, of knowing that she was selling her body for the doubtful privilege of gaining a temporary reprieve from Carl?

She had fled the mountain cabin Brad had taken her to, glad that he had suggested they drive up there separately, but she hadn't gone back to the apartment. Instead she had driven to the coast and found a cottage motel on the beach, quiet and secluded, somewhere she could think without fear of interruption. And she had decided to stick to her original plan and come home here where her roots were, to the father who would understand without words that she needed him. . . .

Now he wasn't there. The shock was so great that she reacted with anger. How could he not be there when she needed him so badly? For the first time in her life he had failed her. . . . She became aware of Bridget's hand shaking her shoulder, Bridget's voice as it penetrated her consciousness.

'Nat? Natalie!' Then, farther away, her despairing words to the stranger. 'Dear God, the child is in shock!'

Booted feet crossed the floor, and Natalie felt her head being snapped up by rough fingers under her chin, then a stinging slap administered none too gently to the rounded curve of her cheek.

Pain shot through her, accompanied by a spurt of anger. How dared this stranger strike her, Natalie Forman, in her father's house? Her breath sucked in on the swell of her temper and she leapt to her feet.

'Who the hell do you think you are?' she snapped, facing up to the man who towered over her above-average stature. He wasn't even good-looking, she noted with scornful awareness. His features seemed carved of brownstone, his nose far from regular, his chin too aggressively thrust forward in his lean face. His skin had the texture of badly smoothed leather, his lips hard lines without fullness. His deep-set eyes were the brown of a boiling river stirred to its depths by spring run-off.

'Now, Nat,' Bridget began nervously, 'don't speak to Cal that way. He's——'

The man called Cal quelled her with a look, which he then turned on Natalie.

'My name is Calvin Hendricks, and I've been taking care of the ranch for your father for about six months now.'

'My father hired *you*?' she spat scornfully. 'What

strong-arm tactics did you use on him? Dad would never willingly let another man run the ranch for him.'

'You haven't been here for a while, have you?' the rough voice gentled slightly. 'After your mother's death Doug lost the will to live. You see,' his voice dropped almost to a whisper, 'he'd lost his daughter, too, long before that. She was too busy with her city career to even come and comfort him when her mother died.'

Instant denial sprang to Natalie's lips, only to be stilled as fast. Why should she be put on the defensive by this odious man? 'My father understood my reasons at the time,' she said with cold venom, 'but I wouldn't expect a hired man to understand or even be interested in the personal lives of his employers. In other words, Mr Calvin—whatever your name is—it's none of your damn business!'

'It could be more than you think,' he retorted, his voice controlled as he moved to the door. He addressed Bridget from there. 'I'll be in for supper at seven.'

Natalie's jaw was still dropped in amazement when his denim-clad hips, neat under the taut material, disappeared from view. Instantly she rounded on the housekeeper and demanded, 'Who does he think he is? Anybody would think he *owned* the ranch, the way he acts!'

'Don't take on so, child,' soothed Bridget, moving back to the stove and opening the oven door to extract a covered casserole dish. 'Indeed, your father would have been in sorry straits if not for Cal these past months. He had no heart to carry on, you see.'

The only sound breaking the silence that fell over them was the chink of the porcelain lid being removed from the casserole. As the familiar smell of Bridget's stew wafted across to her, Natalie felt tears prick at her eyes.

'You blame me too, don't you?'

The older woman sighed. 'Who can blame anybody else for doing what they feel they have to? You'd made your life elsewhere; the old can't hold the young from what they choose to do, and your father was the last one who would have wanted to keep you here against your true inclinations.'

Natalie stared at the back of the untidy, greying head, noting subconsciously that there was more white than the black Bridget had always sported. Time went on, however hard you to tried to push it back; death came, taking away the ones who were needed most. She slumped back into the chair and said numbly.

'What's going to happen now, Bridget? I needed Dad so much right now, and he—he's not here. What am I going to do?'

Giving her a hastily appraising look, Bridget replaced the lid and returned the casserole to the oven. 'You're not alone, child. You've got me—and Cal. He'll run things for you until you decide what you'll do with the ranch.'

It wasn't the ranch that had been on her mind. She had never taken much interest in its day-to-day running, only sure that with her father at the helm it would continue its prosperous way. A way that had provided amply, if not luxuriously, for their needs. Her concern at that moment was more for the need that had driven her back here, back to the parent who had always understood her, always restored the pride that had been buffeted from time to time over the years. He alone had seemed to know and discount the wilful part of her nature, the part others had labelled imperious, self-serving, even arrogant. Only Doug Forman had seen right to the soft centre at the heart of her. Even her mother had remonstrated with him at times, even Bridget. . . .

Now there was no one, never would be anyone who cared for her in that special way. Her head dropped to her arms on the tabletop and gasping sobs began to rack her. Tears came, hot scalding tears that had little of healing in them. Bridget's warm hand on her shoulder was comforting but restrained, as if the older woman sensed her need to release grief in the time-honoured way.

Later, when the hiccuping sobs were further spaced, she said quietly, 'It was what he wanted, darlin'. He could never have been happy again without your mother, rest her soul.'

Natalie raised her blotched face and said with a spark of her old spirit, 'He had me! He loved me!'

'Yes, he did. But the love for a daughter can never be the same as a man's for a woman.'

Man's love for a woman! Natalie had seen precious little evidence of that kind of romantic attachment in her years in the city. The men she had come in contact with had mostly been anxious for a quick affair, hoping their wives safely stashed away at home taking care of their children wouldn't find out. Or the other kind, unmarried yet wanting the best of what marriage provided without the responsibility of commitment. It was true, her parents had instilled in her a rosy picture of what true love could be, but that kind of romantic idyll had died with them and their generation.

'I'll get my cases,' she said with a despair that lay badly on the almost perfect symmetry of her features. Bridget looked anxiously after her as she went to the door and disappeared into the square central foyer of the house. Then, realising it was better to leave her to work out grief in her own way, she sighed and went back to cooking the evening meal.

In the hall, Natalie almost stumbled over the smallest of her three suitcases and she stared numbly down at its gold hide contours. Someone had gone into her car and brought her luggage. But who? It seemed too thoughtful a gesture for the brusque man who had made no effort to hide his contempt for her.

Dismissing the problem, she picked up the light suitcase and went along the corridor branching to her right, reaching the bedroom that had been hers all her life and seeing the larger luggage propped conveniently for easy unpacking. Definitely too courteously attentive for a man of his calibre.

The tall, sparse figure came back to her as she went farther into the room and dropped the small suitcase on the creamy surface of the heirloom bed-spread. Who was he? He spoke with too much authority to be a hired man, yet hadn't her father written to tell her that he had hired someone to take care of things for a while? Why would a man like him, so obviously used to giving and not taking orders, be working in this part of the world helping out a sick rancher?

Her movements were listless as she snapped open the biggest of her cases and started to unpack the hastily thrown in assortment of clothing, adding them to the rack of things she had left behind in the wall-length closets. Her hand stopped, then lingered on a tan satin sheath dress. It had fitted her like a glove, smooth and sleek over the high points and rounded curves of her figure.

Even as her fingers caressed the cool, dully glinting material a frown positioned itself between her eyes. She had been wearing this dress on the night Murray had told her he was marrying Janice, who until then had been her best friend from toddler years.

Jan ... blandly wholesome Jan of the tow-coloured hair and baby blue eyes, her sturdy figure inherited from her stocky rancher father. Even now, three years later, anger stabbed painfully at Natalie's heart. How could Murray—dark, handsome, almost too perfect Murray—bear to think of marrying anyone but herself? Everyone had been expecting just that after two years of pairing off, of being seen together at every function in their Valley community, of the quarrels that had split them from time to time only to end in ecstatic reconciliation.

Except for that last rift that had left Murray open to the schemes of other Valley girls, even the unlikely Jan. Jan who had fought vicariously the battles between her best friend and the man she had, amazingly, always coveted for herself.

'You said you could never marry a man like Murray,' she had told Natalie when faced with her wrath a day later. 'You said he was spineless, that you wouldn't marry him if he was the only man left in the Valley.'

She'd said that before, but Jan had never taken her seriously. This time she had with the consequence that she, not Natalie, was now mistress of all she surveyed at Ridgewood. Ridgewood with its big, turreted turn-of-the-century house, its flowered and forested grounds, its thousands of acres devoted to raising the best beef cattle in British Columbia's hinterland. Pride had rescued Natalie from the humiliation of squabbling with Jan over a man they both loved in their own ways.

Only her father had witnessed the storm of outraged tears, the recriminations for both Jan and Murray. His voice still seemed to echo in this very room.

'I know it hurts now, honey, but try to face facts. You'd never have been happy with Murray, he's not man enough for you. You need somebody strong and firm, who won't be influenced by considerations like money or property.'

Strangely, it had been easier to bear after that. Murray had always been influenced by his parents, who in their turn were influenced by the size of Jan's family holdings bordering theirs. It hurt less to know that Murray had opted for the better material prospect, and not rejected her as the desirable girl she was.

Natalie dropped her hand from the dress and moved back to the suitcase. She hadn't stayed for the biggest wedding the Valley had seen in years; that would have been too much to expect. Instead, she had taken off for the excitement of the city, con-

fident of her ability to make it there, to be a sparkling
success in a world far removed from the Valley.
Maybe she had wanted to come back triumphant,
proving to Murray that he hadn't wrecked her life
by marrying Jan, that men important in the world
of business found her attractive, desirable.

Maybe she had even thought of bringing a suave
man of business with her, a husband strong and firm
as her father had prescribed. Her shoulders lifted in
a dismissing shrug, then she was overwhelmed again
by her loss.

Falling on the creamed smoothness of the coverlet,
she gave vent to tears which, this time, healed even
as they spilled.

CHAPTER TWO

Sun fell in yellow bars over her bed when Natalie
woke the next day, her first morning at the ranch without the presence of her father forming a familiarly
safe background to the ranch day. Forgetting
momentarily, she stretched under the covers, a half
smile forming on the voluptuously formed bow of
her mouth.

The rough male voice biting out the day's orders
was as familiar to her as the butter crunch quality of
the morning. In her mind's eye she could see her
father, hear his early morning rough voice telling
Will, Jerry, Buck what he wanted done that day.

'. . . I have some business to tend to this morning,
so I won't be up there until afternoon . . .'

Natalie shot upright in her bed, the smile fading
abruptly from her sleep-tousled features. That wasn't
her father's voice, it was . . . She sprang out of bed,
her bare feet soundless on the thick carpet as she
sped across to the lace-draped window.

Outside, a little distance from her room, Cal
Hendricks stood with his back to her addressing three
men, only one of whom she recognised: Buck. The
other two were young, as Jerry and Will had been,
their denims tautly fitting over slim hips. Buck was
from sturdier stock, chunky in grey and blue check
flannel shirt; his hair was grizzled now, she noticed

as he lifted his wide-brimmed hat to scratch thoughtfully at his head.

Venom hardened her eyes as they came back to Cal Hendricks again. The confidence expressed in his broad, compactly muscled shoulders and tapered hips in matching beige-coloured outfit set her eyes blazing with renewed hatred.

It had been almost seven the night before when she had wakened from the exhausted sleep her weeping had led her into, and she was palely composed—numb really—when she had made her appearance in the kitchen. If she had thought about Cal Hendricks at all, it had been a fleeting hope that he would already have eaten his supper and taken himself off to wherever he called home.

But he had been there at the spread kitchen table, his dinner only half gone. He made no concession to politeness when Natalie came into the room, apart from laying down his fork at the side of his plate.

'Oh!' The hooded eyes flickered over her when she made clear by her involuntary exclamation that she had not expected him to be there. She was stupidly aware of his male scrutiny over the close fit of her coral blouse and well cut white slacks. To Bridget she said, 'I'll—just have a tray in the living room, Bridget, don't bother to lay the table.'

'It's no bother, child,' Bridget hesitated on her way to the stove, 'I just thought you might like some company tonight.'

Tonight! From now on, without her father, she would need company every night. But not the stranger's.

'I'd rather be alone, Bridget, thanks.' She moved

in the direction of the stove. 'Carry on with your dinner, I can fix some for myself.'

The harsh voice spoke for the first time. 'I think Bridget's right, you shouldn't be alone tonight. Stay here and eat with us.'

Invitation or command? It sounded like the latter, but Natalie was too weary to argue.

'All right,' she capitulated abruptly, waving Bridget back to her seat opposite Cal. 'I'll serve myself—please?' she added to the hovering house-keeper who would, she knew, heap her plate with food it was impossible to eat right then.

Even the spoonful of aromatic stew she served on the warmed plate would choke her at this moment, but she carried the small portion to the table and seated herself with unconscious dignity at the head of the table, Cal on her right, Bridget on her left.

'That's not enough to keep a sparrow alive,' the latter complained, eyeing the infinitesimal amount Natalie had served herself, then she subsided after an imperious glance from the abnormally subdued girl.

'From the looks of her,' Cal interposed, his eyes again touching on the narrowness of her waist, 'she's been living that way for quite a while.'

Anger whipped her dulled spirits into a semblance of their usual ardour. Rounding on Cal, she said icily, 'I eat a perfectly normal diet ordinarily, Mr— Hendricks, not that it's any of your business. And speaking of that,' she stared directly into the clay-coloured eyes, 'there's no need for you to stay around here any longer, now that I'm home.'

Thick brown eyebrows lifted in sardonic enquiry.

'You think you can run a ranch this size on your own?'

Natalie had the grace to drop her gaze from the penetrating knowledge in his. 'It won't be necessary for me to run it. I intend to sell the ranch immediately.'

Bridget's disbelieving gasp sent a faint surge of irritation through her. What had she thought, that Natalie herself would carry on where her father had stopped? It would be difficult for a woman who knew what she was doing, let alone an ignoramus on ranch matters like herself.

'You'll be taken care of, Bridget,' she affirmed crisply. 'It's time you retired anyway, you've . . .' She had intended to tell the housekeeper that she had worked long and hard for the Forman family and deserved a carefree old age, but Cal Hendricks interrupted her in a voice so furious that she blinked in momentary nervousness.

'Bridget has no need or desire to retire for a long time yet,' he cut in brusquely. '*I* need her here, if no one else does.'

'*You*?' Natalie stared back at him, her eyes tawny brown pools in her paled face. 'I've just told you, *you're* not needed around here any more! My father——'

'Your father,' he gritted, 'forestalled you. He's already sold the ranch.'

Her eyes grew wider, disbelieving. 'You're lying! He would never have sold it, he loved it, he's always been here. He'd never dream of—selling the property.'

'You did,' he returned smoothly, yet anger still

burned deep at the back of his eyes. 'You lived all your early life here, yet the first thing you want to do is to sell it.'

She blinked again, then stared down at the untouched food on her plate. That was different—wasn't it? She had never had the abiding interest of her father in the place. Yet she did love the ranch in her own way, the freedom that was unknown to city people, the satisfaction of knowing that the hard work her father had always known was used and appreciated by the hundreds of people he fed by his efforts. But . . .

'Who bought it?' she questioned dully as she wrestled with the sudden feeling of loss. 'Murray Elson?'

'I'm not at liberty to say.'

Her head reared and her eyes flashed fury at him again. '*You're* not at liberty to say? Who the hell do you think you are anyway?'

'I'm someone your father entrusted with the running of his ranch until such time as the purchaser can make payment,' he retorted evenly. 'Which won't be for another six months or so, so you'll just have to kick your heels waiting for your inheritance, won't you?'

'I'll see Dad's lawyer first thing in the morning,' she stormed vindictively, ignoring Bridget's half raised arm of protest.

Unperturbed, Cal rejoined smoothly, 'As you wish, but I believe you'll find everything in legal order. And I'd like to correct your order of events for tomorrow. First, you should visit the cemetery and the graves of your parents. I understand you've never been to your mother's grave either?'

Revulsion spurred Natalie's leap to her feet. How could she visit that cemetery on the hill outside town, seeing the graves of the people nearest and dearest to her? She would want to crawl in beside them, to lose herself as they had.

'No!' she said violently, pushing her chair away as she stepped back from the table. 'I—I can't.'

'You can,' he looked up at her commandingly. 'If it's only as a gesture to your father's memory, you'll go. Doug set a lot of store by what his friends and neighbours thought, and he'd want that.'

'He wouldn't! Daddy never wanted me to do anything that would . . . She stopped abruptly, aware suddenly of how the words would sound to this nasty excuse for a man.

'Upset you?' he filled in for her snidely. His tightly drawn lips expressing his contempt, he pushed back his chair and rose to his feet, standing close to Natalie and sending a shiver of apprehension though her with his looming height. 'Maybe he should have made you do things you didn't want to do sometimes, dusted the seat of your pants more often! He just might have made a woman out of you!'

Eyes snapping, Natalie stared with loathing into the deadly brown eyes. 'You're such an expert in child rearing that you dare criticise my father's raising of me? I'll tell you something, Mr Hendricks—if you had *ten* daughters who jumped to do your bidding, not one of them would have for you the love that I have—had—for my father!'

Bridget was on her feet too now, her hands making futile gestures in the air towards the two of them.

'God forbid that I should be saddled with ten female offspring,' he retorted, not without a wry touch of humour in his fleeting, ironic smile, 'but if I was burdened in such a way, I'd guarantee that not one of them would turn out to be a spoiled, arrogant little brat!' He swung away, saying over his shoulder to Bridget, 'I'll have my coffee in the living-room.'

Spoiled, arrogant little brat! . . . He meant she was that way, of course, and anger broiled somewhere under Natalie's skin. His understanding of her nature was as superficial as most of the people she had come in contact with over the years. Understanding! Why should she expect understanding or any kind of consideration from a man of his calibre? With an impotent gesture of her hands, she turned to Bridget. 'God help his children, they don't stand a chance!'

'That's a silly remark if ever I heard one,' Bridget recovered a measure of her stolid forbearance. 'It would be surprising indeed if he had children, and him not married!'

Not? Natalie gazed thoughtfully in the direction Cal Hendricks had taken. She had taken for granted, subconsciously, that such a man would have been claimed long ago by a woman bearing a streak of masochism—how else could a woman bear to have her every movement monitored and censured, as she was sure Cal's wife would have to endure? The soft bow of her mouth twisted in wry reflection. What woman in her right senses would feel a compulsion to marry a man like him? Obviously none, as his unmarried state proclaimed.

'Will you be having your coffee in the living room too?' Bridget interrupted her meditations, her button eyes falling to the untouched plate of food at Natalie's place. 'Though you'd be better to eat something substantial than fill your stomach with no nourishment at all.' Bridget was notorious for her disdain of caffein-filled coffee, though she brewed the best cup in the district.

'When does Cal Hendricks leave?' Natalie asked, her mind obsessed with a need to be alone, apart from Bridget, in her father's house.

'Leave?' The housekeeper seemed bemused. 'Cal doesn't leave, child. He lives in the house.'

Natalie moved away from the window area and went thoughtfully back to the warm cocoon of her bed, yet the covers were nowhere near the creamy smoothness of her bare shoulders as she sat up hugging her knees under the blankets. Cal Hendricks was a thorn in her side that she would have to deal with. A visit to her father's lawyer should soon clear up the misunderstanding about the ranch. It wasn't possible that Doug Forman had sold the property to some nameless purchaser. He wouldn't have done that, she knew. He would have waited to see what Natalie wanted to do with it, leaving it to her judgment. What Cal Hendricks had to gain by leading her to think that the ranch was out of her control she didn't yet know. But Henry Purdoe would.

She decided that the morning's excursion would take them only as far as the lawyer's office. The thought of visiting gravesites was abhorrent to her, even the resting places of her dearly loved parents. Maybe if she hadn't cared so much for them she could face the cold impersonality of their graves, but in her memory's eye they were both still living, viable people, not corpses slowly disintegrating in the confines of funeral boxes. Doug wouldn't have wanted her to go there, to grieve . . . he would have wanted her to remember him, her mother, as they had been in life.

She was ready when Cal, still dressed in his beige outfit, brought round to the front of the house a car that was strange to her. Probably his own, she reflected dully as she accepted his ironically courteous ushering into the pale green interior.

'I called Henry Purdoe earlier this morning,' he told her as he settled himself familiarly behind the wheel. 'He's expecting us at eleven.'

Natalie glanced at the slim gold watch on her wrist. 'Eleven? It's only a quarter to ten now, and it doesn't take an hour and a quarter to reach town.'

'No,' he returned easily, accelerating down the sandy driveway, 'but we have a call to make first, remember?'

'I've told you,' her voice was low, furious, 'I don't want to go to the cemetery! I—I want to remember my parents as they were, alive, loving . . .' Her voice choked on a sob, and the brown eyes flashed for one compassionate moment in her direction before going back to the front.

'Alive?—no, they're not alive. Loving?—who knows? Do you believe in a life that goes on after death?'

Breath caught and strangled in her throat. She had never had occasion to wonder if some part of a person survived in the void left by bodily death. Even at her mother's passing, if such thoughts had

occurred to her she had pushed them away out of
sight. Strange that it was now a man like Cal
Hendricks who had brought up the subject so
casually, easily that the concept was easier to com-
prehend, less threatening to the part inside her that
habitually denied any facet of life which brought discomfort.

'I've—never thought about it,' she told him hesitantly, not sure even now if she wanted to change
that state of affairs. She felt his eyes on her again
and lowered her lashes to obscure the internal
churning she was sure must be reflected in her expression.

'You've lost your mother, now your father,' he
went on relentlessly. 'Don't you think you should
face up to those facts and maybe wonder a little, as
most people do when someone close to them dies?'

Her lips compressed, she made no answer.

'All right. Suppose there is an after-life, and that
your father knows what's going on with you right
now. Would you want him to believe that he raised
a daughter so tied up in her own dislike of unpleasant
things that she can't even visit the graves of the
parents who loved her?'

Natalie drew a shuddering breath as the car slowly
entered the hillside cemetery gates. 'Why don't you
mind your own business for a change, Mr
Hendricks?' she challenged shakily. 'My parents
knew I loved them in life.'

'But not in death?' he taunted, and drew up to
the risen mound of still-fresh flowers and wreaths.
'You're scared even to get out and see where they're
laid to rest, aren't you? You might have to think

about other people's feelings instead of just your own.'

Her fingers fumbled with the door catch and swung the heavy metal outward almost before the jibing words penetrated. What gave Cal Hendricks the right to judge her and her actions?

Her scramble from the car landed her at the grass verge bordering the grave that held both of her parents, and Natalie drew up short, her eyes widening as they took in the lavish display of floral tributes to her father. Greenhouse blooms of red and white carnations, pink bud roses liberally interspersed with white gypsophila, freesias contrasting with the more definite yellow of trumpet lilies. She stooped lower, reading the cards attached to the wreaths and crosses. The Fowlers, the Harbens, the Legion's offering of red, white and blue, even a simple bouquet from Murray and Jan Elson. There were flowers, tributes, from all the people Doug had known all his life, as well as a sprinkling from newcomers to the Valley. The stiff outlines of marguerite daisies was softened by the green of feathery fern; the card, when she bent farther to expose it to view, read simply: Cal.

Tributes from everyone who had known and loved Doug. From everyone except . . . Her eyes pierced the outer floral display to the dark earth below. 'I loved you too, Daddy,' she whispered, her eyes filling with the hot scald of tears. 'I just didn't know . . .' She drew herself up, clasping her slender hands tightly before her. No words she spoke now would reach the man who had loved her so deeply and so well, despite what Call had said. How could there be an awareness after death? She couldn't see, feel or sense the presence of the man who had loved her so much. Cal's beliefs were an illusion, odd in a man so factually orientated, yet . . . Something of Doug, of Joanna his wife, lingered and became personified in this simple country graveyard. They had returned to the earth they had nurtured and cared for in their lives.

Then like a dream, an illusion, her father's voice came to her, gruffly concerned as she had heard it many times. 'Don't fight so, honey. What's to be, will be, however we try to alter the course of life. Accept, don't kick against the traces . . .'

The voice was so real, so tangible that Natalie's head lifted to search for its source. There was nothing; only the neatly ordered graves pressing in on either side. A hoarse cry broke from her, one she didn't recognise as her own.

'Dad? Daddy, where are you? I need you, I love you.'

The tight feeling in her chest erupted into hoarse, racking sobs. Unbearable pain seared her, and she bent without strength to the heady fragrance of the hothouse blooms, a devastation inside her telling her that the loss of her father, her parents, was more than she could bear.

Strong arms scooped her up, pressed her sobbing head to a chest that was comforting despite its hardness. Her reasoning told her that it was Cal who held her, Cal who ran a comforting hand across the soft spring of her hair, Cal whose voice murmured the words she wanted, needed to hear. But it was some strange flip of her heart, a quirk of the nature she had only barely acknowledged before that made her aware of the erotic effect of his man's body cradling hers. Shocked by the force of sensuality surging through her, she lifted her head to stare bemusedly up at him.

She saw in stark relief the hard line of his jaw clenched to tightness as if he, too, was aware of the unfamiliar sensations flooding her being. The hawk-like contours of his face suddenly took form and made an unbelievably attractive composite, one her tawny eyes went wonderingly over. He was all-male, all-beautiful . . . her eyes closed when his head bent inexorably towards hers. A mindless urgency softened the lips she raised to the hard lines of his.

They were hard when they touched the flower softness of hers, the simile enforced by the heady fragrance of the blossoms around them rising to her nostrils. She felt their hardness and the almost immediate softening, a pliability that sought, claimed, and sought again. Dear God, what was happening to her? A strange man was holding her in his arms, above the new grave of her father, and she was responding in a way she never had before. The high peaks of her breasts swelled and pressed to the iron wall of his chest, her hips clung fluidly to the firm stance of his thighs.

Uncontrollable longing pressed her pliant body against his, as if she sought to immerse herself in the hard male strength of him. The full bow of her mouth opened under the pressured assault of his lips. She clung closer, feeling his instant rejection as a personal affront when he clamped his hands on her shoulders and thrust her from him.

'Don't try to find your salvation through me,' he told her harshly, roughly, as he pushed her to arm's length and held her there, the coral slash of her lipstick smeared round his mouth. 'Look for somebody to cling to if you have to, but don't make it me.'

Humiliation scraped rawly inside her as she stepped back and stared into the eyes that had become hard as river pebbles. Had she really imagined that his granite features had taken on an overwhelming attractiveness just before he kissed her? Before he kissed her ... that remembrance brought a small measure of balm to her shattered ego.

'You kissed me, remember?' she jeered coldly, stepping round him to reach the passenger door and pausing there, her hand on the chrome handle, to look scornfully back at him. 'You're the last man in this world I'd look to for anything, so don't concern yourself on my account!

She swung the door open and bent her body gracefully into the car. Cal stared hard after her for another moment, then went round to his own seat and got behind the wheel. His mouth was a grim line when Natalie glanced at him minutes later, unnerved by his implacable silence. Then, shrugging, she unzipped the soft brown leather of her bag and took out her cosmetic case to repair the tear damage to her face. If he wanted to sulk, let him sulk!

It was only as they were passing the first straggling houses outside the small town that he broke the silence.

'I have time to do some business at the bank before

we see Purdoe, so why don't you have some coffee
and I'll pick you up at ten minutes to eleven.'

It was more of a statement than a question, a
command rather than a request, but Natalie stifled
the protest that rose automatically to her lips. She
needed to pass some time, and at least she didn't
have to pass it in his company.

He drew up in front of Cardera's coffee shop, the
more élite one of the two in town, the one with che-
quered red cloths at separate tables and a few booths
lining one wall. Natalie got out without a word, and
Cal offered none to her.

Tightlipped, she walked across the sidewalk and
pushed open the latticed glass door, a faint smile
curving her mouth when she heard the jangle of the
old-fashioned bell above it. Cardera's was the haunt
of the conservative set in Holden, the young people
preferring the more garish attractions of Phil's Diner
further down the street. Cardera's suited her mood
of the moment, though; she wasn't up to running
into old friends and acquaintances right now. Too
much was on her mind, not the least of which was
getting rid of Cal Hendricks from her life.

Selecting an empty booth at the darkened rear
end of the café, she dropped into the section facing
the door. A quick glance at the few other patrons
told her that none of them posed a threat to her
privacy, and she breathed a faint sigh of relief. She
wasn't up to facing some of the old bats who had
been her greatest critics in her teen years. She wasn't
so lucky in the waitress who came to serve her.

'Natalie Forman? Good grief, where did you
spring from?' Trudy Welburn, as fair and softly

round as ever, widened her china blue eyes incredulously. At school she had always half envied, half
admired the bolder Natalie's exploits. Her eyes
clouded instantly. 'Oh, I'm sorry, I guess you came
because your father di—because of your father,' she
tacked on hastily.

'Yes.' There seemed no point in explaining the
true circumstances to Trudy, who had always
thrived on drama. 'I'm just sorry I didn't get here
in time.'

'Yeah, it was too bad,' the blonde girl commiser-
ated, her eyes making a quick check on the perfect
cut of Natalie's white wool suit. 'I guess you're doing
real well in the city, huh?'

'I—work for an advertising agency.' What point
would there be in telling Trudy that she had been
fired from her job on the very day of her father's
death?

'Really?' she breathed, then sighed extravagantly.
'You've really hit the big time, Nat, haven't you?'

Irritated, Natalie's expression froze as she glanced
at her watch. 'I have an appointment soon, Trudy,
so do you think you could bring me a coffee?'

'Oh, sure, right away.'

Showing her hurt at being dismissed so abruptly,
Trudy hurried away and Natalie silently cursed Cal
Hendricks for dropping her off here. She could have
waited in the car while he completed his bank business, and she wouldn't have been exposed to Trudy's
prying—and she wouldn't have lied about still
having her job at the agency.

That thought led to another. Nobody here knew
that she was a failure in the big city of opportunity.

She had confided in no one, not even Bridget. Had she subconsciously been looking for a safe retreat from Cal Hendricks and what he represented? She smiled her thanks when Trudy placed the coffee before her, but something in her expression must have warned the other girl off, because she made no effort to linger and talk. So she had made another enemy—what did it matter?

Cal Hendricks did matter. Not because he had kissed her; she dismissed that idea out of hand. She had been kissed before, and in all likelihood would be again. It wasn't that that bothered her about Cal. It was his sureness that he had sole concern of her father's affairs that lay like a thorn in her side. Her father had stipulated that he, Cal, was to take charge until such time as the unknown purchaser could take possession.

Unknown purchaser . . . who could it be? Surely, if it was Murray or any of the local people, there would be no problem, they would take over as soon as a decent interval had passed. The thought insinuated itself into her mind that the purchaser might be Cal himself. But how could an itinerant like him come up with the considerable sum she knew would be needed to purchase a property like Blue Lake Ranch?

Another thought penetrated and left her breathless. When the mysterious purchaser came up with the funds in six months, or whenever, she herself was heiress to a tidy fortune. She had never given much thought to the day when the ranch and all it entailed would be hers; it had been too important to prove, to herself and others, that she could make it on her own, be a success in her own right.

Strangely, the thought that in a matter of months it wouldn't be important whether she ever became a commercial success on her own account left a sour taste in her mouth. She wouldn't have made it by her own efforts, but by the unremitting labours of her father and his father before him.

The coffee, good and strong as Cardera's always was, slid down her throat. She would have money enough to travel where she liked, to live where she liked, yet it was as bitter gall to her. What was wrong with her? Ninety-nine people out of a hundred would be more than happy to stand in her shoes. Was Cal right? *Was* she a spoiled brat who had everything yet wanted more?

Her glance shifted to the door when the tinkling bell announced another arrival, and her eyes narrowed against the brightness outlining a man's figure as he strode to the counter where Trudy presided. Her heart leapt and turned, knowing with fatalistic certitude that Murray had come in, that he was joking with Trudy at the counter. Natalie's eyes roamed hesitantly, then hungrily over the near perfection of his dark features, the jet of his carelessly brushed black hair, the almost noble outline of his straightly carved nose and well moulded chin. Even as her eyes lowered to the wide set of his shoulders under red plaid jacket, panic had set up a fluttering in her pulses.

He was the same Murray she had always loved, had always known as intimately as she had known any man. Her hands had smoothed, clung to the shirt covering the hard muscles of his chest, had run through the thick coolness of his black hair, had delighted in teasing him to near madness before skipping away and laughing at him throatily.

Now it was Jan who had licence to run her fingers through his hair, to incite him to the passion he no longer had any need to control.

She saw Trudy's red mouth intoning words into his ear, the quick turn of his head, the narrowing of his eyes to penetrate the shadows surrounding the booth where she sat. Adrenalin pumped its flight message through her veins, but she remained statue-still as he came towards her, his ranch boots dull thuds on the whisper soft carpeting.

'Nat?'

Her lips formed a smile, the trapped smile of a rabbit watching its predator fate approaching. What was the matter with her? She had long ago consigned her romantic dreams of being Murray Elson's wife to the flames of self-destruction. It was inappropriate, useless, to let them rise again now.

'Hullo, Murray,' she forced the greeting through stiff lips. 'I didn't expect to see you here.'

She had meant in the Cardera coffee shop, but he seemed not to take her up on that meaning.

'Not half as surprised as I am to see you in Holden!' His voice still had the same warm intonation she remembered, and she was still pondering that thought when he went on, sounding embarrassed, 'but of course you've come because of your father.'

Natalie nodded, her thick tawny brown hair bouncing slightly on her shoulders, her eyes misting as they met the soft brown of his. 'Yes.'

Murray dropped into the seat opposite, his long-fingered hands dealing abruptly with the zipper on his jacket. 'I'm really sorry, Nat,' he told her soberly, 'I know how much your dad meant to you.'

Warmth eased the aching pain of loss inside her and spread up through her body to reach the cold tips of her fingers. Murray's words were the first comfort she had known. It seemed right. Murray had always recognised that special bond between her and her father.

'I—don't really believe it yet,' she said huskily, lowering her lids though her eyes wanted to taste, devour the new maturity in him. It was there, from the freshly carved lines beside his full lips, the fan of tracery round his clear eyes. 'I—couldn't get here for the funeral.'

'No.' Hesitantly, he met her eyes and went on, 'I guess you've made a busy life for yourself in Vancouver.'

'Well. . . .' She still wanted desperately to make him know that her life hadn't ended with his marriage to Jan. 'They tried to get in touch with me, but I had a weekend appointment with a very important client. I work for an advertising agency, you know, so—it's very necessary that I—keep the ball rolling, so to speak.'

She was sounding stupid, inane, but Murray seemed to accept her words at their face value.

'Yes, I can see that,' he nodded sagely. 'It must have been quite a shock to you when you found out about—your father.'

Natalie felt an uninhibited urge to scream. Shock was a mild term to describe what she had felt when she had been told of her father's death. But that was the way country people, ranch people, would describe her feelings, and Murray was nothing if not a country boy. She understood him, even loved him for his homespun concern.

'Yes, it was a shock,' she said soberly, lowering her eyes until they lit on the capable outline of his hands. Those hands had caressed her budding female body, had stirred the beginnings of passionate desire. 'But I don't want to think about it now. Tell me about you, and—Jan.'

'She'll really be glad to know that you're back in town,' he said earnestly. 'Jan's always been fond of you, Nat.'

Fond? So fond that she stole the only man who had ever meant anything to her from under her nose? No. Jan wasn't fond—just a little apprehensive when she found out that Murray's first love was back in town?

'I guess you must be a proud papa by now?' she forced a lightness she wasn't feeling into the normal words any acquaintance might have asked. 'You always wanted a family, didn't you?' The import of her question hit them both simultaneously, and Natilie lowered her eyes to the depleted coffee cup in front of her. It was wrong, out of place, for her to recall, even by insinuation, the plans she and Murray had once shared.

'No,' he said tersely, 'we don't have any children yet, but that's something we're hoping to remedy any time now.'

Her startled eyes reached up to his, reading in the clear dark depths Murray's embarrassment that his marriage had so far proved fruitless. Whose fault? she wondered involuntarily. Not Murray's; if any man was meant to have children it was him. Jan? Despite the illicit thrill of pleasure that ran lightly through her, Natalie knew that her erstwhile friend was, always had been, destined to mother a brood of offspring.

'These things take time,' she said belatedly with a knowledge that far outstripped her experience in matters of fertility. Changing the subject adroitly, she brightened her tone. 'I've been thinking about having a get-together at Blue Lake one of these days, and I'd like you to come—Jan too, of course.'

Irritation swept hotly over her when Murray hesitated and seemed embarrassed by her suggestion.

'You don't have to come,' she said stiffly, compressing her mouth when Trudy came with Murray's coffee and replenished her own.

'It's not that, Nat,' Murray offered contritely when the fair girl had left them after a curious glance that encompassed both of them, 'it's just that—well, isn't it a little soon after your father's—? I mean, you know how people talk around here, and I wouldn't want them to put you down in any way.'

'Put me down?' She stared blankly, not understanding. 'The town gossips have always put me down, and always will.' Light dawned then, and she gave a brittle laugh. 'Oh, you mean because of Dad? Heavens, Murray, I wasn't planning on having it next week! Even if I was, Dad wouldn't have minded, you know that.'

Murray regarded her soberly, then spooned sugar into his coffee as if relieved to have an excuse to look away from her. 'Yes, I know that, but . . .' His face brightened as a thought struck him. 'I have a better idea. It's Jan's birthday in a couple of weeks, and I've been thinking about throwing a surprise party for her. Nobody could say anything about you attending that, and you could maybe even help me plan it. You've lived in the city for so long now, you must know a lot more about parties than anybody here. How about it, Nat?'

Coping with the varied flood of emotions washing over her, Natalie made no reply for long moments. Was it really possible that Murray was sounding like one of the old witches who had done all they could to make life miserable for her because she had plunged wholeheartedly into a life they had long forgotten or never known? But it wasn't fair to make that kind of judgment. Murray had been brought up in that same small town environment, had never been away from it, so it was natural that their prejudice had rubbed off on him. It hurt, though, that where he had once been as scornful as she he now seemed to embrace their bigoted outlook. Apart from that, there was a searing, and unexpected, jab of piqued envy. It was ironic, really, that the man who had loved her so madly once was now asking her to arrange a party for the wife he had chosen for materialistic reasons.

'I don't know, Murray,' she hedged. 'I don't even know where I'll be next week. From what I hear from Cal Hendricks, I don't know if I'll have a home at all when the new owner takes over at Blue Lake.'

Her tentative probing brought immediate response. 'New owner?' Murray puzzled, the dark frown between his brows enhancing his rugged handsomeness. 'You mean you've sold the ranch already?'

Natalie shook her head. 'Dad beat me to it, it seems. He sold it to somebody who can't produce the payment for another six months or so. As a matter of fact, I'm waiting for Cal Hendricks now to go see Henry Purdoe.'

'I didn't know about the sale,' Murray said so bewilderedly that she knew Elson money hadn't been involved in the transaction, 'but you couldn't have anyone better than Cal by your side to take care of your affairs. He's a great guy, Nat.'

Her head reared and her eyes flashed a yellow glow at him. 'You're well acquainted with him?'

'I wouldn't say that,' he prevaricated uncomfortably, seeming to sense her antagonism where Cal was concerned, 'but he's pretty well been running Blue Lake for the past few months, and your father seemed to trust him. He's very well liked in Holden, Nat.'

'Really!' Natalie looked around the table area as if searching for gloves she didn't have. 'It seems as if I'm on my own as far as he's concerned!'

'What's wrong, Nat?' Murray leaned across the table, his hands capturing and holding her fluttering ones. 'Don't you feel you can trust him?'

Too conscious of the touch of his skin on hers, Natalie could say nothing though her eyes spoke volumes as they roved over the familiar good looks. Why, her heart cried, why had he thrown away the love that had been between them? She knew, from the half caressing hold on her slender-boned hands, that Murray had no more forgotten what had been between them than she had. His fault, not hers. Jan had offered more materially, but could that make up for the true love she felt for him?—*had* felt, she corrected automatically, though a sinking feeling inside her doubted the death of that love.

Her eyes reflected the molten glow of autumn sunlight as she stared deep into the eyes across from hers. 'Murray, I . . .'

'I'm sorry to interrupt,' a familiarly harsh voice splintered the fragile words trembling on her lips, 'but we're going to be late for our appointment if we don't leave right now.'

CHAPTER THREE

NATALIE looked up, meeting the bland stoniness of Cal's eyes as she disengaged her hands from Murray's grip. Instead of the guilt feeling he obviously expected, a swift burning anger shot through her. What right did he have to make a judgment, biased or otherwise, on her actions? Not that the action of being touched, held, between Murray's sensitively long fingers had been of her own initial volition. Nevertheless, she hadn't withdrawn her hands from his and an outsider might have thought . . .

What did it matter what Cal Hendricks thought? Rising, handbag in hand, she said coolly, 'I doubt if Henry will be bothered by a few minutes' delay, unless business is booming a lot more than it did in my day.'

'A lot of things have changed since your day,' was his rejoinder, hurtful in its pointed sarcasm. Temper flared under her collected exterior when, after a brief nod in Murray's direction, he led her to the door, fingertips pressuring the sensitive bones at her elbow. Why did he always arouse this urge in her that wanted to hurt, to rebel against him?

'I'm quite capable of seeing Henry Purdoe on my own,' she snapped viciously as the Cardera's tinkling overhead bell sounded their departure. 'In fact, I prefer to conduct family business without benefit of outsiders.'

A strange feeling of fright invaded her senses when she saw the hard tightening of the pugnacious jaw, but following close on its heels was the certainty that she was within her rights to see her father's lawyer in private. What she wasn't prepared for was Cal's abrupt release of her elbow, his curt, 'Very well, if that's what you want. I'll be waiting in the car outside his office when you're through.'

Conflicting emotions chased their reflection over her features as she watched him walk away, tall and slim and, to her eyes, arrogantly confident. An angry sigh escaped her as she turned in the opposite direction and traced the half block to Henry Purdoe's office. From him, at least, she could expect straight-from-the-shoulder talk.

Half an hour later she was standing in the lower hall of his upstairs legal office, too paralysed to take the few extra steps to where she knew Cal Hendricks waited for her.

What the hired man had told her was all too true. The ranch had been sold to a purchaser not even Henry Purdoe was privileged to name. And Cal, the man she was beginning to hate with every fibre of her being, was to be in charge until such time as the new owner could take possession.

'Surely I have the right to know who the buyer is,' she had stormed to the man who had been her father's lawyer since the beginning of his practice in Holden.

'No, Natalie, you don't,' he had told her with unaccustomed firmness, his cherubic pink-skinned face topped by flying wisps of pure white hair. 'It was your father's wish that you shouldn't be bothered with details. As you know, he never wanted you to be distracted from your busy life in the city. And of course he had no idea when he made this codicil to his will that he wouldn't be here to implement it himself. I believe he had planned to buy a smaller house here in town.'

Biting with sudden fury on her soft lower lip, Natalie looked through the unfrosted glass panes of the door to where Cal, supreme confidence etched in every inch of his rugged profile, waited for her. That confident air infuriated her further. Why should he, a stranger, enjoy the security her father had provided for him, even if it was only for a half year?—while she, Doug Forman's daughter, had to kick her heels and endure some mediocre job in Vancouver. The house they shared was just as much her home as his; more so. Her roots were here, she had lived in that house all her life until three years ago. Why should she let Cal Hendricks usurp her place there?

A man in Western clothes looked curiously at her as he pushed into the building, and she tightened her grip on the bag under her arm. Blue Lake Ranch belonged to her until the new owners took possession; she was boss there, not Hendricks.

His hooded eyes flickered knowingly over her as she threw herself into the seat beside him and slammed the passenger door.

'I see you've found out I wasn't lying,' he observed drily, one big hand reaching for the ignition key.

'No, you weren't lying,' she said abruptly, smoothing the white wool of her skirt across her knees.

'So?' he quizzed, making no attempt to set the car in motion. 'Do I take you to the nearest airport or back to the ranch?'

Natalie threw him a venomous glance, her eyes a yellow smoulder. 'The ranch, of course. Why should I need an airport?'

'I just thought you'd want to get back to your important city job as soon as possible,' he drawled casually before glancing into the rear view mirror and pulling out into the centre of the main street.

Her eyes swivelled back to the sidewalk where people strolled unhurriedly. In Vancouver, at this time, the early rush for lunch would have started.

'No. I've decided to stay on here for a while.'

'Oh?' She felt his eyes rest speculatively on her profile for a moment before he turned back to the traffic line, then he said softly, 'You never did say why you came back just at the time you did.'

Natalie's breath drew in sharply. She couldn't recall having been asked why she had chosen to come back to Blue Lake the day before, but in any case it was . . . 'My reasons have nothing to do with you, Mr Hendricks. Believe me,' she mocked, 'If I'd thought they had you would have been the first one to know.'

His uncaring shrug infuriated her, and she turned sharply back to the side window where the small frame houses, each with its acre or so of ground surrounding it, flashed by as Cal picked up speed outside town. Was it one of those that her father had had his eye on for his retirement? Her eyes misted with tears. How he would have hated the confinement of one acre after a lifetime of unlimited space at the ranch! Strangely, the thought soothed her hurt slightly; Doug had died where he had lived, as he must truly have wanted it.

She hadn't been aware of the slide of tears down her cheeks until a large-sized male handkerchief was thrust on to her clasped hands in her lap. About to protest that she had her own blotting material, she subsided in her seat and dabbed furiously at her cheeks. She couldn't have trusted her voice at that moment.

'Correct me if I'm wrong—and I'm sure you will!—but my guess is that things weren't all you'd cracked them up to be in the city. All those things you wrote to your father . . .'

'*You* read them?' she asked incredulously.

'Doug was so proud of you, he wanted me to,' he returned equably. His eyes swivelled quickly to her again. 'He didn't see what I saw in them; a woman must have to sacrifice quite a few of the principles she might have to get ahead in that kind of business.'

Natalie's mind went quickly back over the infrequent letters she had sent to Doug. Apart from mentioning an upcoming business dinner with an account executive, she couldn't recall that she had written anything that might have been construed as compromising to her morals—and that was what Cal was suggesting.

'You're really behind the times,' she laughed huskily, her throat still thick with the emotional tears she had shed. 'Things have changed a lot lately, or hadn't you heard? A woman doesn't have to sleep with her clients to get their account now.'

'No?'

There was a world of scepticism in that one word,

a worldly-wise knowledge that very little had really changed in the world of business. A woman could still go further, faster, using age-old methods. That was his thinking, and he wasn't far wrong, she admitted wryly. But she wasn't about to tell Cal Hendricks that he was right, that she had come beetling back to her father because she couldn't stand the pace in the business life of today. Cal was a man of few illusions, she guessed, one used to taking his sex where he could find it. In that way, was he any different from the men who had lusted more for her body than the agency services she offered?

'No,' she returned firmly, and he said nothing more, silence falling between them until they turned into the long driveway leading to the ranch. It was Cal who broke it.

'So how long are you planning on staying?' he asked flatly, negotiating a curve with no lessening of speed.

'Why? Don't you want me here?' It would have given her a perverse pleasure to know that her presence might irk him, for no palpable reason that she could think of.

'It's not up to me to want or not want you,' he told her in the same flat voice as he pulled up in the sandy parking area in front of the house. Cutting the engine, he half turned in his seat to give her a long, level look. 'That would depend on your motives for staying. If you're thinking of stirring up mud in waters long since gone under the bridge, then I'd say no, you should go back to where moral ties aren't so strong as they are here.'

'Just what do you mean by that?' she asked

heatedly, her palm itching in its sudden desire to smack the quiet contempt from his lean-featured face.

'You know what I mean. What was between you and Murray Elson years ago is dead wood now. Don't try to rekindle any flames, Natalie.'

'You don't know what you're talking about!' she snapped, stung. 'Somebody like you could never understand what Murray and I had going for us until his family talked him into marrying Jan!' Aware that she had gone too far, said too much, she subsided into the shape of the bucket seat, her teeth pressing her bottom lip to whiteness. The words had spilled out from somewhere deep inside her and were, she realised with a pang, the truest she had spoken to Cal since leaving the lawyer's office. What had been between herself and Murray was something timeless, something all the wives in the world couldn't alter. That knowledge had flown like an electric current between their clasped hands over the coffee table.

'Jan's a nice girl,' Cal broke quietly into her chaotic thoughts, irritating her unreasonably. 'And right or wrong, she loves the man she married. So don't start something you're not capable of finishing.'

The last words were couched as a veiled threat, and Natalie threw back her head against the pale green upholstery to sneer, 'And what do you propose to do about it if I choose not to hear the gypsy's warning?'

She was unprepared for the quickness of his work-manlike hand, its hard pressure under her chin as Cal turned her face to him. Her eyes blinked ner-

vously as they met the savage coldness in his, and
fear trickled icily down her spine.

'I'm warning you not to ignore it,' he said harshly,
his face so close to hers that his breath fanned warmly
against her mouth. 'If you do——' his eyes narrowed
to slits, 'if you do, I'll have to deal with you in my own
way. And that isn't Murray Elson's lily-livered way.'

Natalie struggled against the close confinement of
his fingers, only to find them tightening more inexorably on her aching jaw. 'Let me go!' she choked,
her eyes reflecting the loathing his touch sparked off.

'When I'm good and ready,' his tone brooked no
arguments from her. His fingers gentled suddenly
and she felt their tips trail provocatively across her
skin to the trembling softness of her mouth. Her eyes
flicked upwards to his and saw the softness begin
there too. 'Not that I can blame any man for wanting what you're willing to throw at him,' he went on
softly, narrowing the gap between them until his
mouth reached within an inch of hers. Natalie com-
pulsively jerked her head back, only to find it im-
prisoned in the cushioned softness of the car seat.

'Leave me alone!' she gasped, shaken by some
nameless terror that left her with unusual weakness.
Locked into her seat by the overpowering presence
of him, she knew that she was the prisoner of this
man who had her at his mercy, broad daylight or
not. The impulse to scream was stifled in her throat
when he spanned that last inch between them and
laid his mouth to hers.

Frantically her eyes rolled sideways to the house,
which lay still and quiet under the midday sun, then
on to the equally deserted stockyards and corrals

adjoining the house. Panic fluttered through her when she realised that Bridget would be preparing lunch in the kitchen at the back of the house, and the men Cal had issued instructions to early that morning would be far up into the hills.

Her eyes closed on the loathsome realisation that Cal's mouth was bruising hers, pressuring her lips in a way that forced them to part and give him access to their delicate inner surface. Unwelcome sensations rippled through her, a weird mixture of wanting him to stop yet wanting him to go on. On to what? The answer to that was so shocking that she found from somewhere deep inside her a superhuman strength that brought her hands against the hard warmth of his chest and forced him from her.

Panting, she stared into the eyes that had become repulsively familiar to her. Repulsive—yet his features seemed to have taken on again that aura of attraction she had noticed earlier in the cemetery. In reaction, her eyes sparked hatred at him.

'Do you always find it necessary to rape a woman to get her attention?'

His body stiffened and straightened away from her, his eyes resuming their pebbled hardness. 'Rape?' He laughed harshly and leaned back against her to say with soft menace, 'If I were that kind of man you wouldn't be sitting there squawking about rape after one little kiss. And no,' he shifted away from her, only his eyes pinning her to the seat now, 'I've never found it necessary to use force for women's favours. But that's a state of affairs that can change,' he added hardly, 'If you start stirring up those waters I mentioned.'

Natalie fumbled for the door catch, her fingers stiff. 'You're crazy! What business is it of yours, how can it possibly matter to you if I stirred up every marriage in the Valley?'

'It doesn't matter one bit to me,' he shot back so harshly that she believed him, 'but it would have mattered to Doug, and that's good enough for me.'

Having pushed the door open, Natalie turned back to look at him disbelievingly. 'It's my father you're thinking of? How very touching! You and he must have become very close friends in your short stay in the Valley.'

'Something like that,' he replied evenly. 'Let's just say that I don't like to see a good man's faith go to waste.'

Disdaining an answer to that one, Natalie stalked into the house. Calling to Bridget that she was home, she went to her room and closed the door behind her with a sigh of relief. The man her father had hired to take care of the ranch was impossible, arrogant, too confident, dangerous . . .

She walked to the dresser mirror and stared meditatively at herself, her fingers coming up to touch the bruised outline of her lips. Yes, he was dangerous. Any man who resorted to brute force was dangerous. Nothing about him was attractive to her as a woman. She wanted, needed, a man of sensitivity, a man who would understand her as her father had understood. A man like—Murray.

Turning away restlessly from the mirror, she told herself it was useless to think of Murray in any other way than a good friend from the old days. Cal was right in that, she admitted reluctantly as she un-

buttoned her close-fitting white jacket and
skirt, hanging them neatly in the closet before
reaching for jeans and yellow tee-shirt. What had
been between her and Murray *was* water under the
bridge, water that could never be recalled.

And yet . . . how was it possible that that same
awareness lay between them that had always been
there? She had recognised it right away. The
pleasure she had felt in his dark good looks, his
pleasure in seeing her again. Nothing had really
changed. Only Jan lay between them as an obstacle
that should never have been there. And who could
she blame for that? Not Jan, not Murray, but herself.
If she had taken the first step towards patching up
their differences, instead of letting stupid pride stand
in her way, she and Murray would be married now,
not Jan and Murray. And they would have had at
least one child by now. A child to inherit the
Ridgewood acres, a son to bear the Elson name. John
Elson after Murray's father, a boy rich long before
he knew the meaning of the word. And in time there
would have been a daughter, sharing, like her
brother, the looks of her parents.

'Natalie?' Bridget's voice closely followed her
knock on the bedroom door and Natalie turned
bemusedly towards it as she called out for the housekeeper to come in.

'What is it, Bridget?' she asked edgily, pacing to
the dressing table to pick up a hairbrush, stroking it
through the thick mane of her hair as Bridget hesitated on the threshold.

'There's been quite a few phone calls while you've
been out,' the older woman told her, her eyes tender

scant three years after their marriage. 'He has that same way with him, that—understanding so many men lack.'

Understanding! Natalie would have guaranteed that Cal Hendricks' understanding extended only as far as making sure that his own personal satisfactions were fulfilled. But the hired man wasn't uppermost in her mind at that moment.

'Bridget, did you know that Daddy sold the ranch before he died?' she enquired curiously.

'Well,' the older woman replied uncomfortably, 'I did hear something to that effect.'

'And doesn't it worry you that the new owners won't want you around here?'

Bridget's cheeks drew down ominously. 'Now where would you be getting an idea like that? Your father, and Cal himself, have assured me that there's a job for me here as long as I want it.'

'It's one thing for them to say that, another thing altogether for the new owners to feel the same way,' Natalie said tartly, feeling an immediate pang of compunction when Bridget's face fell into depressed folds. Hastily, she added, 'But that's really not something *you* have to worry about, Bridget. Housekeepers like you are few and far between these days. They'll probably thank their stars that they've inherited a jewel like you.'

'That's as may be,' Bridget sniffed, her old self-confidence restored. 'It's possible I won't care for them, and there's no reason why I have to stay with people I don't like. Your father left me well provided for, gentleman that he was.'

That much was true, Natalie knew, because of

her visit to the lawyer's office that morning. The same warmth that had filled her then at her father's generosity flooded back to her now. Bridget had been a member of the Forman family for so long, had cared for his ailing wife in her last illness, had nurtured his beloved daughter.

Through the lump in her throat, she said huskily, 'If we're having supper that early, I don't need much for lunch. I'm not used to eating ranch-style meals, Bridget.'

The older woman's eyes went disparagingly over the whip-lean contours of her stomach and hips, ignoring the deep swell of fully formed breasts under the yellow tee-shirt.

'That I can see very well. You need some good home cooking to build you up to what a woman should be, but——' her bright button eyes took on a probing look, 'I suppose you'll be getting back to the city as soon as you can, having your job to go back to.'

Conscience smote Natalie. She should tell Bridget, sure of her understanding, that the important job in Vancouver no longer existed—had it ever, except in the eyes of the people who loved her? Cal Hendricks hadn't been impressed by it; in fact, he had seemed to look right through her thick veneer to where she was hurting badly because of her failure in that glamorous, important job. But would Bridget understand, any more than she had understood the wilful nature of years ago? No, the housekeeper was as straight and uncompromising as she had been then.

'No, I've decided to give that up,' she said coolly, straightening her hairbrush and turning away from her dressing table. 'Dad might have sold the ranch out from under me, but there's no reason why I shouldn't stay here among my friends until the new people take over.'

Bridget's undisguised pleasure stayed with her uncomfortably long after she had left the room telling Natalie her lunch would be ready in fifteen minutes. Yet why shouldn't she, as she had told Bridget, remain here with lifelong friends as long as possible? So, Murray Elson was here, but he wasn't the only friend from the old days. There was Jan. Although their lifelong friendship had ceased abruptly after the announcement that Jan, and not she, would marry Murray, they must still have lots of things in common. They could laugh again at the outdated prejudices of the upright, honest citizens of Holden, mocking the disapproval that followed Natalie's actions like a black cloud. There was Gary, and Linda, and Art, and Jason, and—oh, dozens of people in the old gang.

Her spirits lifting, Natalie smoothed down her jeans and gold sweater and went out with appetite to the lunch Bridget had prepared for her.

It was only after two hours of telephoning, being welcomed enthusiastically back into the fold, that Natalie realised Jan's name had been omitted from Bridget's scrawled list of callers. As she sat at the hall table beside the beige-coloured phone, her brow knitted thoughtfully. Did Jan think that she, Natalie, still held a grudge because of what had happened three years before? The euphoria she had felt after the genuine pleasure of her other friends ebbed swiftly away. Jan had been her friend for longer than any of them, yet now they were poles apart because of a man, Murray. Admittedly, a man who had re-stirred her senses fleetingly in Cardera's coffee shop, but that had been a momentary thing, a flashback to early days when she and Murray had been free to love each other in the way of young people.

Picking up the phone decisively, Natalie dialled the well-remembered number, drumming her fingers nervously on the aged wood of the desk top as she listened to the ringing tone. Every woman in the world, she reflected sagely, must remember her first love with a wistful catch at her heart. Must wonder what might have been if . . .

'Hello?'

'Jan? It's me, Natalie.'

'Oh. I heard you were back in town, and I was going to call you.'

The lukewarm words, spoken in an even cooler tone, sent a flash of irritation through Natalie. She wasn't holding any grudges, so why should Jan?

'I met Murray in town this morning, did he tell you?'

'Yes, he—said he'd had coffee with you at Cardera's.' Why the hesitancy? Natalie wondered edgily. 'I'm—sorry about your father, Nat. It must have been a shock to you to come home and find out something like that.' Without waiting for an answer, the breathless voice rushed on, 'I guess you'll be getting back to the city now. That's too bad, be-cause I would have liked to see you again, to talk over—old times.'

'We'll be able to do that,' Natalie returned

smoothly. 'I've decided to stay on until the new people take over the ranch.'

'But what about your job?' Jan ejaculated so swiftly that Natalie's mouth twisted in irony. 'Surely you have to get back for that?'

'I can always pick up where I left off,' she returned glibly. 'There are a few things that need to be tied up in connection with the sale,' she lied with equal facility.

'Yes, of course.'

Of course! The business aspects of tying up an estate would be perfectly comprehensive to Jan, who had been auctioned off to the highest bidder in marriage. For the first time, Natalie wondered if Jan had been more influenced by her parents than the love—and it had been sudden—she bore for Murray. If that was so, then the marriage was a sham, a false front for the merging of two vast properties.

'Let's meet,' she said impulsively, warmly. Apropos nothing, Cal Hendricks' leanly sombre face hovered before her eyes. He had accused her of trying to stir up the dead embers between herself and Murray. What could be more contradictory than having Jan visit her here at the ranch? 'Come and have lunch with me tomorrow.'

'Tomorrow? Well, I—yes, all right.' Jan's final agreement was tinged with misgiving, and irritation spiked through Natalie again. Was Jan so unsure of her hold on Murray that she dreaded contact with an old girl-friend of his? When the phone was still in its stand after arrangements had been made for Jan to come about eleven-thirty the next day, her thoughts winged far out from the familiarity of the spacious hall surrounding her. Married to Murray, would she herself have been so obviously uncertain to meet one of his old flames? No, she vowed inwardly. As Murray's wife, mistress of Ridgewood, no other woman could have threatened her.

There was something of cool defiance in her statement that night at the early supper, Cal on her right, Bridget on her left. 'Oh, by the way Bridget, I've asked Jan to come for lunch tomorrow, is that all right with you?'

Bridget beamed. 'Of course it's all right. It will be like old times, sure and it will, to have you and Jan chattering like magpies in the house again. I'm glad that you're letting bygones be bygones,' she laid a pressing hand on Natalie's, 'and not harbouring a grudge against that dear girl. She and Murray are very happy, I believe.'

A faint wince of pain crossed Natalie's features, then her eyes met the mocking brown of Cal's. 'Why should I hold a grudge? After all, you have to admit that Murray made a good match in Jan.' Brightly, brittly, she carried on, 'She had a lot more to offer than I ever had.'

'Maybe what you were offering was too much for him to handle,' Cal interposed brusquely.

Natalie widened her eyes. 'You think so, really? I must confess that he never gave that impression when he and I were an item years ago. He could never get enough of me. You remember,' she appealed to Bridget, some impish devil driving her on, 'Murray and I were never apart for very long.'

'That was a long time ago,' Bridget said with unusual vehemence. 'You were both very young.'

'And very much in love,' Natalie added softly, the tiger yellow of her eyes turning to rest on Cal's tightlipped expression as she sighed, 'But that's all in the past now. He's married to Jan, and marriage is sacred, wouldn't you say, Cal?'

'I doubt if what I say is of any importance to you,' he returned abruptly, pushing back his chair and rising to his feet. 'In fact, I doubt if what anyone else says is of importance to you. You seem to me to be one of those people who go by their own rule-book. But remember,' the brown eyes rested hardly on her upturned face, 'the rules you go by could bring more sorrow to yourself than anyone else.'

'Do tell, Cal,' she mocked. 'I'm sure your experience outweighs mine by a bushel or more. Where will my rule-book let me down?'

'Whenever you consider your own welfare more important than other people's,' he retorted harshly, his figure looming largely over the table. 'And I'd guess that's a lot of the time.'

Stung despite herself, Natalie lashed back, 'And who's going to be the judge of the rules I live by? You? You're a man of mystery, Cal,' she jeered. 'No one knows where you came from or where you go from here. Does your knowledge come from personal experience, or do you just talk from the top of your prejudiced head?'

Bridget's outraged gasp was drowned in the ring of Cal's heels over the kitchen tiles. At the door, he turned and lashed Natalie with his eyes.

'Just hope,' he said tautly through his teeth, 'that you don't have to find out the hard way.'

CHAPTER FOUR

It was nearer to twelve than the eleven-thirty they had arranged when Jan drove up to the ranch the next day. Natalie, trim in butter yellow shirt and brown cord slacks, went forward from the overhanging shelter of the porch to greet her. Two car lengths away, she stopped and appraised her old-time friend with surprise.

The figure emerging from the energy-conscious VW had thinned down over the intervening years. In fact, Jan had changed in more ways than one, she recognised as the other girl hesitated, then came towards her. The tow-coloured hair was now a matt golden colour, Jan's slightly square face enhanced and thinned by the application of make-up. Her pants-suit of azure blue perfectly matched the shade of her eyes, and only the uncertainty reflected in those eyes made Natalie aware that the other girl was indeed her erstwhile friend.

'Hi,' she said warmly, her arms briefly circling the shapely form outlined under the blue material. 'I'm so glad you came.'

Jan returned the pressure of cheek on cheek, then looked curiously at Natalie's features. Her voice, when it came, was as lightly breathless as it had ever been.

'Hello, Nat. You look as beautiful as ever.'

'Beautiful?' On impulse, Natalie linked her arm with the other girl's and drew her towards the house. 'What happened to all the straight talk about pimples and blemishes?'

Jan's eyes went in a blue haze over the flawless skin. 'You don't have any now.'

'Praise be!' Natalie said so fervently that both girls looked at each other with the familiarity of old friends who had shared the acne of youth and so many other things besides. 'Do you remember when my face was like a relief map of China?'

Laughter joined them as they reached the heavy wood of the ranch door. A warm river of memories swept between them, engulfed them as they stepped into the wide coolness of the hall.

Attracted by the mirth, Bridget stepped out into the hall, her face breaking into a delighted smile when she saw Jan. 'Sure and I never thought to see the pair of you together again like this—at least, not in this house.'

'Why not?' Natalie cried, her eyes dancing from the rightness of it all. She linked her arm to Jan's and drew her to the arched entrance of the living room. 'We've always been friends, and we always will be. How about some tea, Bridget—or maybe I'll pour us some sherry?' she enquired of Jan, her hair bouncing silkily at her nape as she looked at her long-time friend.

'Anything,' Jan said faintly, the carefree smile fading to leave recently traced lines round her wholesomely full mouth, an etching beside her blue eyes. She halted half way into the room, pulling away from Natalie to say, 'I'm—really sorry about your

dad, Nat. I know you and he were—that you were
always very close.'

Instantly sobered, Natalie went to the buffet side-
board and reached for the sherry and glasses. 'I don't
know what I'm going to do, Jan,' she said starkly,
her fingers trembling slightly as they poured amber
liquid into hard cut crystal. 'Dad was the only one
who knew—who cared—about me. Nobody understood me like him.'

'Isn't there anyone in Vancouver?' Jan received
the well filled glass and looked searchingly into
Natalie's eyes. 'You must have met lots of men there,
Nat. Isn't there one who——?'

'There isn't one,' Natalie returned briefly, carrying her glass to the far end of the room where she set
it down on a side table before dropping with unconscious grace into the black leather of an armchair
flanking the fireplace. 'Not one I'd be interested in,
anyway. They're different, Jan, from the boys we
grew up with here. Most of them want all the bless-
ings of marriage without the hassle of providing for
a wife and children. In fact,' she lifted her glass and
took a healthy gulp of the pungent liquid, 'most of
the men I came in contact with were married
already. I was just a sideline.'

Jan stared at her from where she had taken the
seat opposite, her fingers clutched whitely on the
stem of the sherry glass. 'You make me feel so guilty,'
she whispered, dropping her eyes from the straight
look in Natalie's. 'If you'd stayed here and—married
Murray, you'd have been happy.'

'Don't be foolish.' Natalie drained the last of her
sherry and rose to pour another, undeterred by Jan's

still full glass. 'Murray chose you. That was what he wanted then, and it's what he wants now.' The words tripped out of her glibly, speaking not of their truth but her inexplicable desire to set Jan's mind at ease. What point would be made in persuading Jan otherwise? What had been between herself and Murray lay far back in their youth. He and Jan were married now, a tie that was indissoluble in the Valley. No one was interested in any mistakes that might have been made. Right was right, and wrong was—wrong.

Wrong! Was it wrong to feel this bittersweet regret that her life had no apparent purpose, no pre-ordained meaning? Hadn't she been born in this valley, destined to live out her life here with a man like Murray? The sharp bite of the sherry pursued its course down her throat.

'Murray needs children,' Jan said with a deadly calm, lifting her glass to her lips and draining half of its contents at one gulp. 'I'm not able to give him those children, Nat,' she said starkly, looking at the sherry before tossing it back into a receptive throat. 'He needs a son, and I can't give it to him.'

Natalie stared at her, her mind whirling. 'Of course you can give him a son,' she heard herself saying. 'You haven't been married that long. Give it time, Jan.'

'Time?' the other girl echoed with a hollow laugh. 'We've been married for three years, and all the doctors can say is that the operation I've just had will make it possible for me to have a child. Possible!' she ended on a half sob. 'No guarantees . . . just a

possibility. Oh, Nat, I'm worse than useless as
Murray's wife. Maybe he should have married you.
You'd have given him a son long before now.'

The words were torn from her childhood friend,
just as the avowals that Natalie was more popular in
their childhood had been wrung from her in
moments of despair. Now, as then, the words were
an accurate description of their disparate states.
Natalie *had* been the popular harum-scarum one of
the duo, just as now she . . .

'Murray loves you,' she comforted now, her hand
lighting on Jan's firm shoulder, knowing with Valley
wisdom that she lied as she went on, 'What does it
matter that you haven't given him a child? It's you
he loves . . .'

'Oh, Nat,' Jan straightened and sniffed at the tears
thickening her breathing, 'you're a good friend. To
think,' she smiled tremulously, her hand coming up
to clasp Natalie's on her shoulder, 'that I was
worried about you and Murray—that you'd both be
thinking how much better off you'd be with each
other.'

'Murray and I had a thing going,' Natalie acknowledged briefly, straightening away from Jan and
going back to the empty chair by the fireside, 'but
that was over long ago, Jan. He wasn't really my
type, was he?' she posed facetiously, settling herself
again into the commodious chair by the fireplace. 'I
realised that as soon as I got to the city. I need a
man who's important in his own right, a man I can
respect . . .'

Her words tapered off there, the realisation borne
in on her that Murray was such a man. Important

in his own right, a man she respected above all others. But she couldn't say that to his wife, the woman who had pledged to devote her life to him.

Jan was looking appraisingly at her. 'What about Cal?' she queried in the same way they had discussed possible males in their teens. 'He's the kind of man even you could respect, not to mention that every girl in shouting distance wants to tie him down.'

'Cal?' Natalie dismissed the thought scornfully. 'A woman would have to be desperate to look on somebody like him as a husband!'

'Nina Fourchette doesn't think so,' Jan retorted, seemingly forgetting her own qualms about Natalie and Murray in her newfound interest in Cal Hendricks. 'She told me he's the sexiest man she's ever met.'

'Huh!' Natalie responded automatically. 'Only somebody like Nina could be attracted to a self-centred egotist like him!'

'Cal?' Jan seemed puzzled. 'He's never struck me as being big headed. He's always seemed to me the kind of man a woman could depend on, especially if he—well, if he was fond of her.'

Fond of her! Great balls of fire, Natalie fumed, didn't she even know that a mild emotion like fondness has no place in Cal Hendricks' make-up? That a woman who wanted him would have to accept the thorn as well as the rose of his abrasive personality? From her own experience, it needed little imagination to conjure up the kind of woman who would appeal to a man like him. A woman with enough earthiness to supplement the demanding maleness in his nature, a compliance to the masculine dominance he would demand in his woman.

'I wish Nina luck,' she said briefly, and quite obviously changed the subject to a more neutral point of interest. 'I hear that Jason and Linda are a twosome these days . . .'

The conversation centred around those and other old acquaintances while they ate the lunch Bridget had lovingly prepared, though Natalie's thoughts were mainly on the people most closely concerned with herself. Murray's darkly handsome features interposed themselves between her and Jan, bringing a nostalgic remembrance of days long past. While Jan's lips moved, Natalie tried to picture Murray's clearcut mouth kissing them in the ultimate intimacy of the marriage bed, and failed miserably. Much more clear in her mind was the yearning of his body towards hers, the oneness that should by rights have been theirs. Oh God, was she destined to go through life haunted by the thought of what might have been? Why had Jan come between them, as much a failure as a wife as she had been as a popular girl with Valley boys? Not even her softly confided, 'I love Murray so much, Nat,' made sense in Natalie's mind as she went with her friend to the parking lot in front of the house.

'Come for lunch tomorrow,' Jan urged at her car, her eyes dumbly clinging to Natalie's. 'Murray's always away in the daytime, and I get lonely.'

The prospect of another solitary lunch with Jan held little appeal. While Natalie was still struggling with that thought, Cal's rough male voice said from behind them,

'What's it like to have nothing else to think about but inviting friends to lunch?'

'Cal!' Jan turned to face him with undisguised pleasure. 'If I didn't know you'd refuse, I'd ask you too.'

'Lunch is a little out of my line,' he admitted, his feet soundless on the soft sandy soil as he came to stand, deliberately or by accident, at Natalie's shoulder. 'But I wouldn't say no to dinner tomorrow night if you asked me.'

Jan laughed her delight. 'You don't leave me much choice, do you? All right with you, Nat?'

Dinner in his company held even less appeal than a solitary lunch with Jan, but a refusal would have sounded churlish in the extreme—besides, Murray would be there.

'Fine,' she responded coolly, stepping back when Cal gallantly went forward to open the driver's door of Jan's car. 'What time?'

'Oh, around seven. We'll have a drink or two before dinner.'

Keeping the stretched smile on her face as Jan got into the car and backed before surging forward down the driveway, Natalie was only too aware of the well-knit figure of the man beside her. Her hand lifted in a farewell wave, then she swivelled on her heel to go back into the house.

'Have a good visit with your friend?' Cal asked conversationally as he fell into step beside her.

'Of course.' She turned to face him as they reached the front entrance of the house. 'Shouldn't I have?' she challenged.

'Why not?' he shrugged, lifting the broad sweep of

his shoulders in an encompassing shrug. 'You've been friends for a long time.'

Long before, his tone implied, Murray and Jan had been married and made their lives at Ridgewood. A Ridgewood still without the patter of tiny feet.

'Yes, we have,' she said crisply, her hand reaching for the ornately carved iron door handle.

'A lot of things have changed since then.'

Natalie turned the yellow sheen of her eyes on him. Jan's words flitted through her brain. Nina Fourchette had told her that Cal was the sexiest man she had ever met. That may have been true—for Nina. As far as she herself was concerned, Cal Hendricks had very little to recommend him as a male sex symbol. His looks were too rugged for her taste, he was too blandly sure of himself as a male to hold her interest. To him, male force was everything, as he had demonstrated so palpably earlier. To a man like him there was only one way to overcome a woman's resistance . . . and he had failed miserably as far as she was concerned.

'Things change,' she said carelessly as she turned the handle and pushed the door open. From the framework of old wood she looked back at him. '*Some* things change,' she stressed. 'Others remain the same, no matter how much time goes by.'

His mouth grew thinner as his jaw clenched in an uncompromising line. 'Maybe,' he emitted tightly. 'The trick is in knowing which things change and which can't be recalled.'

Natalie gave a throaty laugh, wanting to annoy him. 'Quite the philosopher, aren't you?' she mocked. 'But as it happens, I'm not in need of your homespun theories. I've turned down men with degrees in that kind of thing, so I'm not likely to be interested in cowboy homilies.'

She had turned into the doorway when she felt her arm caught between his heavy fingers, her body swung round to face him again.

'You didn't turn down too many of them, did you?'

For a long moment she stared unblinkingly into the flat brown of his eyes, then her own dropped deliberately to the spread fingers on her arm.

'That's something you'll just have to guess about, isn't it? Now take your hand off me, and never touch me again. You're still the hired man around here, and don't ever forget it!'

The biting tone in her last words might have been no more than the sting of a gnat. His hand tightened, numbing her arm, and he stepped closer so that his shirt brushed the silky yellow of her blouse.

'That kind of guesswork wouldn't tax my brains too much, I reckon,' he drawled, his breath warm on her furiously upturned face. 'But don't try any of your city ways here, or——'

'Or?' she blazed when he paused, his eyes going lazily over the slight uptilt of her nose and lingering on the generous fullness of her lips.

'Or I'll see to it personally that you go screaming back to your fancy city men.'

'And how are you going to do that?' she jeered, only a faint flicker of her eyes betraying her recognition of the menace in his hard carved face.

'I have my ways.' His eyes narrowed as his voice

dropped lower. 'And I guarantee you'll find them very effective.'

'If yesterday's demonstration in the car was a sample,' she scorned, 'I don't think I have much to worry about! Now let me go. My time is valuable, even if you don't feel the necessity to earn that generous salary the new owner's giving you!'

To her surprise Cal did just that, throwing her arm from him as if it burned his flesh and wheeling away from her across the sandy forecourt. For another moment Natalie stared after him, her fingers rubbing the numbed surface of her arm. She'd had no need for that flash of alarm where Cal Hendricks was concerned. A touch of mockery about his sexual prowess was enough to reduce him to manageable size.

Turning into the house, she pushed away the twinge of disappointment that inexplicably shot through her. She must be sick to interpret his implied threat of physical force as an exciting tingle along her nerve ends.

'Have some more pie and cream, Cal,' Jan urged, smiling when Cal leaned back in his chair and patted his flat stomach wryly.

'Couldn't eat another bite, Jan, after that delicious meal.' His eyes swivelled to where Murray sat at the other end of the square table. 'You're a lucky man, Murray, to have a wife who can cook like this. I'm almost tempted to try the married state myself.' His gaze went innocuously to Natalie, seated opposite, and she felt a flicker of irritation.

'Shouldn't the congratulations go to the hired

woman in the kitchen?' she said waspily.

'Normally it would,' Jan returned quietly, 'but Jean's away right now. Her mother's sick, and she's the only daughter.'

'So you did cook the meal, right?' Cal insisted, his eyes fixed so hard on Natalie's face that she felt the colour rise under her cheeks.

'It's no problem,' Jan said simply, 'I love cooking, always have.'

'Not me,' Natalie put in, her hand going up to push the heavy fall of her hair to one side. 'Even Bridget gave up on me when I was ten, I was so useless in the kitchen.' She had changed a lot since then, she acknowledged inwardly, and had quite a reputation among her friends and acquaintances in Vancouver as a gourmet cook, but why should she give Cal Hendricks the satisfaction of knowing that she cared about her own culinary expertise? He would immediately conjure up visions of lascivious scenes which would inevitably follow a meal served by her to one of Vancouver's immoral males. And, she reflected sourly, he wouldn't have been far wrong *if* her guests had been other than evenly split male and female friends. For business purposes, her apartment had been strictly out of bounds.

Talk drifted to the subject of coyotes plaguing the Valley ranchers for months past, and she let her attention go to the immediate surroundings. Jan had gone for coffee, so for the first time since she had arrived at Ridgewood there was no need to concentrate on social chitchat.

How often she had pictured herself at the head of this table where Jan now presided! The wood-

panelled walls, the ancient dressers and servers, the
long velvet-draped windows would have taken on a
new ambience. Jan had refurbished the room, sub-
stituting gold drapes for the drab brown velvet
Murray's mother had favoured. But Natalie had
envisioned bright slashes of scarlet against the dark
wood of walls, and restoration of the old woodstrip
flooring to its original patina. Her eyes went down
to the thick gold broadloom carpet that covered
every inch of the old boards. Poor Murray, he could
have had a home to be proud of, that people would
come from far and wide to see.

Her eyes went to him at the head of the table, his
head inclined earnestly towards Cal's as they discussed the coyote problem, Cal evidently on the side of
the animals, Murray intent on wiping out the threat
to his livestock.

She lingered on the black sweep of his hair, the
straight pride in his nose, the healthy red of his well-
shaped lips. It needed little or no imagination to
recall the feel of those lips on hers, the urgency they
provoked. It had always been Murray, she recalled
dreamily, who had called a halt before things got
out of hand. Murray. Sweet, gentle Murray.

'Stop your arguing for a few minutes,' Jan chided,
coming back into the room with a laden tray. 'Poor
Nat's been shut out of the conversation, I know, and
it's not very gentlemanly of either of you.'

'I doubt if the massacre of wild animals holds
much interest for Natalie,' Cal interrupted his discourse to say, leaning back in his chair and eyeing
Natalie with a superior air that set her teeth on
edge.

'Getting rid of one pesky coyote isn't exactly a massacre, Cal,' Murray challenged heatedly, ignoring the fluted china cup Jan placed before him. 'All we want is to get rid of this one animal that seems to know every trap we set for him.'

'Sure,' Cal retorted, sparing a fleeting smile of acknowledgment for Jan's offering of coffee. 'But where do you stop? You could kill dozens of animals before you're sure you have the right one.'

'So? As far as I'm concerned the whole coyote population can be wiped out and I'll cheer the day.'

Jan's voice, purposefully cheerful, cut in on the argument. 'Would you like a liqueur with your coffee?' She reeled off a surprising list of potent accompaniments to the fragrantly strong brew, obviously happy when her ploy worked and the two men turned their attention from predators to pleasure.

Natalie felt her censure when, the words seeming to come from nowhere, she said, 'Preserving a species is fine for people who live in high-rise apartments and never even see a bear or a coyote, but those same people would be the first to squawk if their steaks weren't there each night on their tables.'

She was conscious immediately of the attention suddenly focussed on her. Cal's disbelieving raising of his thick brown eyebrows, Murray's gleam of approval.

'You're so right,' he admired, warming her with the brown glow in his eyes. For a moment the others faded into oblivion and there was only the two of them. Tawny eyes meeting sober brown, heart reaching to heart. Oh God, how could she ever have let Jan, sweet simple Jan, become the female focus in his life? She loved him, and he still loved her. Why else would he look at her that way, as if he too wanted to wipe out the intervening years?

Cal's harsh voice drew her reluctantly back from what might have been. 'I'll believe that when I see you pull the trigger after your sights have been set on an animal fighting for survival in a world increasingly dominated by man.'

'You think I couldn't?' she challenged, her gaze lingering only momentarily over his hardbitten features before lighting on Murray's glowing eyes. 'Let me know when you need an extra hand on a coyote hunt.'

Cal's brusque, 'You don't know what you're talking about,' was mingled with Jan's horrified, 'Nat, don't be so foolish!' Words calculated to bring out the stubborn persistence in her nature.

'I mean it,' she said calmly. 'I think Murray's right in wanting to preserve the livelihood of most of the people in the Valley. And that's what predator animals are threatening, isn't it?' she enquired of a stricken Jan, a hard-faced Cal.

It was only later, when she stood on the Ridgewood veranda with Murray, Jan and Cal having made clear their disapproval of Natalie's concurrence with Murray's views by disappearing towards the kitchen with the used dishes from their meal, that she realised how neatly their opinions coincided, how at one she felt with Murray.

'I'd no idea you had such strong feelings about the things that affect us here in the Valley,' he made a preliminary stab at conversation. 'Your dad thought more along Cal's lines, that animals were just as entitled to free range as man is.'

'Really?' Natalie heard the breathy quality in her voice, ignoring it as she drank in the atmosphere of Ridgewood's sweeping veranda and its view over the undulating hills chastely clad in forest green. 'You're not telling me that Dad would have wanted his stock reduced by a wild predator?'

'No, of course not.' Murray waved his hand in an impatient gesture. 'But then, he wasn't as fired up about conservation as Cal seems to be.'

'Is Cal's opinion so important?' she asked on a note of irritation. 'Of course it doesn't mean much to him. He can afford the luxury of caring for the animals that threaten your livestock and that of the other ranchers in the Valley. After all, he's just a temporary fixture here. In a few months he won't even have a job.'

'When the new owners take over, you mean?'

'Yes. I can't imagine that they'll be fired up about keeping on a man who doesn't look at things from a rancher's point of view.' She let her eyes wander over the dimmed green of the Valley spread before them. 'People like him have no conception of what the Valley stands for. Ranchers need the cattle they raise, just as city people need the food ranchers produce.'

'I really didn't know you cared that much,' Murray murmured, his eyes reflecting the glitter of the early spring moon bathing the meadows spread before them. There was a note of awe, of wonder, in his huskily spoken words, and Natalie felt gossamer threads weaving round her throat.

'You've forgotten, Murray,' she said huskily, her eyes slanting upwards and holding the concentration in his. 'I cared about a lot of things. Still do.'

'Nat, I——' Whether by chance or intent his hands came out and fastened lightly on the short sleeves of her tawny silk dress. He seemed about to say something more, and then Natalie raised her face with provocative openness to his. She was un-ashamed of her clear want to feel his mouth on hers, his arms tight around her. It had always been that way between them; it always would.

His head bent and hers came up to meet it. But instead of Murray's warm lips on hers there was the harsh grating of Cal's voice slicing between them and Murray's convulsive thrust against her arms, pushing her from him.

'I think it's time we left, Natalie,' the harsh voice cut through the moonhaze surrounding her senses. 'By the time Jan's finished with the dishes she won't want to entertain visitors any more.'

Murray's hand came up to smooth the dark strands of his hair, though Natalie's fingers had come nowhere near it. 'Jan won't mind,' he said confi-dently, only the flare of his nostrils betraying the tension of the last few minutes.

'Maybe,' Cal returned briefly, his voice filled with gravel,' but I would. She put herself out to give us a great meal, and that's as much as any of us can expect.'

Meaning that I shouldn't expect to steal her husband from under her nose as well, Natalie scorned inwardly, the lash of Cal's eyes full on her. What business was it of his if she and Murray had been about to re-seal the closeness that had always been theirs? Or Jan's? A church wedding and a piece of paper legalising a marriage of convenience were worthless compared to what she and Murray felt for each other. But the heady moment of truth had gone now, dissipated in Cal's untimely interruption. There would be other times.

'All right,' she acquiesced, a small burst of vindictive pride carrying her forward on winged feet when she noted Cal's frowning disbelief at his easy triumph. What had he expected? An undignified brawl with Jan for possession of the man they both laid claim to? Didn't he credit her with more subtlety than that?

'You're not leaving yet?' Jan's query met them in the hall as she emerged from the rear kitchen and they from the low-ceilinged dining room. 'I thought we might play some cards or dominoes, something like that.'

'Cal's anxious to get away,' Murray said abruptly, his mouth thinned to a disgruntled line.

'Maybe next time,' Cal addressed the surprised Jan, his hand so firm on Natalie's elbow that she winced in pain. 'I have some paperwork to get through before the sale tomorrow.'

'Oh, yes,' Jan nodded understandingly, 'the Blue Lake bulls.'

Natalie was still riled when, Cal's hand guiding her inexorably towards the car, they reached its sleekly substantial outlines in front of the house.

'What bulls?' she demanded furiously as Cal handed her unceremoniously into the passenger seat, leaving her to stalk stiffly to his own seat behind the wheel. 'I asked you,' she gritted icily, 'what bulls?'

He put the car in motion before answering with another question. 'Am I to believe you're interested in ranch stock?'

'I have as much right as Jan to know what's going on at Blue Lake,' she retorted furiously, smoothing the silky folds of her dress round her knees with shaking hands.

'Oh, so that's it?' Cal's head gave an infuriating shake of resigned understanding.

'Yes, that's it,' she snapped. 'I might remind you that Blue Lake Ranch is my responsibility, as my father's daughter, until the new owner takes possession. And as it's my——'

'It isn't.'

Her head twisted sideways, her eyes raking his calmly set profile. 'What did you say?'

'I said that it isn't your responsibility,' he returned blandly, his eyes fixed on the winding ribbon of road ahead. 'Your father left the management of the ranch to me until such times as the purchaser can take full possession.'

'That's just words on paper,' she scorned above the powerful hum of the motor. 'If Dad had known I'd be here, there'd be no ques——'

'But he didn't know, did he?' Cal slowed to negotiate a bend, then sped ahead again. 'How was he to know that you'd step completely out of character and come back in your ignorance to take over the ranch?'

Natalie gasped, her fingers itching to draw their tips down his complacently confident face. 'I was brought up on Blue Lake Ranch,' she gritted through clenched teeth. 'It belonged to my father, and his father before him. It's my responsibility far more than it could ever be yours.'

'All right,' he nodded as he slowed one last time to turn the car into the ranch driveway, 'it's all yours. I'll leave tomorrow morning's sale completely in your hands.'

Natalie felt the air deflating rapidly from her lungs. That wasn't what she had meant, and he knew it, darn him! He knew, too, that she wouldn't know a prize bull from a run-of-the-mill stud. But she wasn't about to admit that openly and give him the chance to make her eat crow on her knees.

'That's fine,' she said coolly, her hand on the doorlock as he drew up some distance from the house. Absently, she noted that only the hall light gleamed faintly through the misted glass panels flanking the front door, which meant that Bridget was probably watching television in her rear bedsitting-room.

'Now that we've got the management of the ranch straightened away,' Cal went on, stilling her hand on the door, 'there's another item we have to discuss. Or had you forgotten my warning about stirring up things that are best left in the past?'

Her eyes gave him a feline glint of mockery. 'Was it worth remembering?'

'You tell me,' he said bluntly, his big hands reaching for the furry wrap around her shoulders, pushing it confidently away and touching her shoulders with a firm grip. His skin's heat replaced the warmth of her wrap, but she shivered nonetheless. The same kind of awareness, half dread, half wanting, insinuated itself into her consciousness and her eyes flashed defensively at the lean contours of his face looming over her. The same strange configuration of his features made him almost handsome as his heavy-lidded eyes went lazily over her face, her hair, the jutting thrust of her breasts under the tawny silk of her dress.

'All right, I'll tell you,' she said unsteadily, her tongue moistening the suddenly dry contours of her lips. 'You don't interest me in the slightest, Mr Hendricks. Maybe your he-man tactics work on inexperienced Valley girls, but they won't work with me. I know everything about men from A to Z, so don't think I'm impressed by your cowboy tactics.'

'Is that so?' he drawled, equally unimpressed by her avowal of experience. His left hand lifted, surprisingly light as it traced the rounded flesh over her cheekbones, the rounded outline of her lips, his thumb touching on the white clench of her teeth. 'Then what I'm about to do won't affect you one way or the other—except maybe to conjure up happy memories.'

Natalie stared angrily at him while his head became lower, so near to her mouth that his breath wafted its male fragrance to her. He was stupid, ridiculous, arrogant. Why should he care if a dozen Valley marriages broke up because of ... Her awareness suddenly became centred on what Cal was doing, his mouth taking a leisurely course across the flushed warmth of her cheek, his hand tracing a lazy downward arc over the sharp thrust of her breast, and flashing anger ignited the powder keg of her emotions. The manicured points of her coral-tinted nails swept up and then down hard on the weathered skin objectionably close to her own and Cal's head reared up as he swore with all the potency of his rugged background.

'Just what do you think you're doing?' she stormed, her hands braced against the taut wall of his chest as she felt his yielding. 'I'm not up for grabs by you or any other man!'

'No?' The ground she had gained was lost abruptly as he leaned forward against her, his hand twisting the thick hair at her nape as if it were a roping lariat. 'You could have fooled me when I saw you with Murray Elson a while ago! What's the matter, Natalie,' he spoke her name softly, 'are you missing all those city men you left behind?' A gasp escaped her when his fingers tightened painfully on her hair. 'If so, why choose a married man to fill the vacancy? I have no ties, no wife to be hurt if I indulge my fancy. Why not settle for me?'

'You!' Natalie put all the loathing at her command into the one word, and had the satisfaction of seeing his eyes narrow, hearing his breath drawn in quickly. 'I wouldn't have you if you were served up to me on a desert island! Your kind of rough stuff has never appealed to me, so let me go.' Her head pulled against his restricting hold and pain shot from her hair roots as he refused to release his grip.

'You have a very funny mouth,' he approved grimly, 'but I can think of a much better use for it.'

His head dipped so quickly that she had no time to close her indignantly parted lips so that he took them with an experienced, ruthless carelessness.

Revulsion rose and almost choked her. It was

Murray she had wanted earlier that night, Murray's mouth on hers like this, Murray's hands stroking, caressing the roused peaks of her woman's body, Murray's thighs hardening as he eased her on to his lap, Murray's mouth growing soft to evoke a passion she had never experienced before. Her hands slid over the warm contours of male chest, rising to mesh and mingle with the thick growth of hair above the shirt collar. Murray . . . oh, Murray!

Sanity returned all too quickly when she heard Cal's emotionally roused voice at her ear. 'You certainly are missing those men in the city, aren't you? And they,' his voice thickened, 'must sure be missing you.'

Natalie returned to the reality of what was happening, that a strange man was holding her, caressing her, kissing her as if he had every right to do so. And she must have led him on to believe that . . .

She scrambled from the lap she had sat on so comfortably, so unaware in her stupidity that it was Cal Hendricks, not Murray, who had brought out the responses she had denied for so long. How could she have been so stupid, to let a man she loathed touch her so intimately, to rouse her as no city man ever could! Her fingers reached for and found the door clasp, and she scrambled from the car, conscious only then of the dress that sagged round her waist, the absence of her flesh-coloured bra.

'Damn you, Cal Hendricks!' she gritted through clenched teeth. 'Damn you all the way to hell!' Leaving the door open as she stalked away on slim line heels, clutching her dress to her vulnerably bared front, she heard his mocking parting rejoinder.

'Let me know when you need another substitute lover,' he called after her, 'I'll be happy to oblige . . . again!'

Fuming outrage followed Natalie all the way into the house, across the hall dimly lit and along the passage to her bedroom. There, she savagely divested herself of the tawny-shaded dress Cal Hendricks had made mockery of and stood stormy-eyed before her dresser mirror. Only too clear was the evidence of her arousal, her mouth softly swollen, her eyes slumbrously gleaming, her pink tipped breasts quivering their awareness. Oh God, how could she have let a man like Cal Hendricks affect her to that extent?

Reaching into a dresser drawer, she extracted a neck-high nightdress of obscuring brushed nylon. It was Murray she loved, and nothing a Valley stranger could do would alter that. Murray . . .

CHAPTER FIVE

MORNING brought a new perspective, a new beginning to Natalie's life. That it was Cal Hendricks, not Murray, who came into her waking thoughts was to be expected. She loved Murray, but Cal couldn't be completely discounted. For one thing he had control of Blue Lake Ranch, a responsibility she had never even considered for herself. The sale of stock would have to be left in his hands. Hands that were more competently sure than her own could ever be.

So where did that leave her? As she munched on the breakfast of ranch bacon and ranch eggs which Bridget had brought to her on a tray, Natalie swallowed more than fresh grown products. She swallowed a pride that had been part of her make-up from the first years of her life. After last night, she would be more than happy never to see Cal Hendricks again, but because he knew what he was doing with ranch affairs and she didn't, her pride would have to take a back seat.

Draining the last of her coffee, Natalie pushed the tray to one side and threw back the covers. Better she faced him sooner than later.

Twenty minutes later, having showered and dressed in pale yellow checked shirt and hip-hugging beige cord slacks, she carried the tray into the kitchen. Bridget was washing dishes at the capacious sink under the window facing towards the back of the house.

'Is Cal around?' she asked so abruptly that Bridget swung round to eye her in surprise.

'He's down at the bull pen, getting ready for the sale.'

'Oh.' Maybe, then, he hadn't meant it about handing the sale management over to her. 'What time does it start?'

Bridget glanced at the teapot-shaped kitchen clock on the wall. 'In about half an hour. Why? Are you thinking of being there for it? You've never shown any interest in that kind of thing before.'

'No, I—no, I just wondered. I—thought I might drive into town, and I want to get away before traffic starts coming in for the sale,' Natalie prevaricated. Halfway to the door, Bridget called her back.

'How did your dinner go last night?' The nut-brown eyes were openly speculative.

Natalie shrugged. 'Fine. Why shouldn't it?'

'You didn't mention it, and Cal didn't either—though he doesn't tell me much about his movements. Was the food good?' she asked with jealous pride in her own skill, adding grudgingly, 'Jean McLeod can make a passable meal when she puts her mind to it.'

'Jean's not there, it was Jan who cooked the meal,' Natalie returned impatiently.

'Ah, then it would be a good dinner,' the housekeeper nodded her satisfaction. 'Jan was always a good cook, even when she was young. Murray's lucky to have a wife like her, sure and he is.'

'There's more to marriage than being able to cook

some meat and boil up some vegetables!' Natalie
retorted acidly, and she was already in motion again
when she turned back to the door, pulling up sharply
when she saw Cal's figure framed in the doorway.

'Isn't your jealousy showing a little?' he drawled
with infuriating slowness. 'Jan prepared an excellent
dinner for us last night, and it involved considerably
more than you just mentioned. Bridget's right,
Murray is a lucky man.'

Colour ran up under Natalie's cheeks, belying her
freezing tone. 'Are you in the habit of eavesdropping
on private conversations?'

'Only when I have no choice,' he returned
equably, making no effort to unblock the doorway.
'I came in to tell you that everything's ready for the
sale.'

'The sale?' Her heart sank to the bottom of her
expensive leather casual shoes. He hadn't forgotten
after all, and now she would have to beg him to
manage the sale in front of the avidly listening
Bridget.

'The sale,' he affirmed with a nod of his well-set
head, his eyes glinting under their hooded lids. 'I
believe you expressed a wish to conduct it yourself.'

'Natalie?' Bridget gasped from behind the girl.
'Excuse me, darlin', but you don't know one end of
a bull from the other, let alone what price they
should fetch.'

Drawing a deep breath, Natalie raised her chin to
look Cal straight in the eye. 'That's what Mr
Hendricks is employed to do,' she said cuttingly. 'I
simply meant that I would supervise the sale.'

'But I thought you said——?' Bridget began,

puzzled, and Natalie whirled on her heatedly.

'I'm going into town *after* the sale, Bridget,' she snapped. 'You must have misunderstood me.'

The housekeeper's mouth dropped at the blatant lie, then, closing it sharply, she turned back to the sink.

'Good,' Cal inserted smoothly, 'now we've got that settled, maybe we should get down to the stockyards.' He straightened up from where he had been leaning on the doorpost and drew something from his pocket. 'By the way,' he said to Natalie, 'you left this in my car last night.'

From the thick roughness of his workmanlike fingers dangled the cobwebbed wispiness of her flesh-coloured bra. The high colour of temper in Natalie's cheeks deepened to a painful brick red. How could he be so tactless as to let Bridget know in this overt way that he had made love to her so intimately? Love! she scorned as she tore the offending garment from his fingers and rolled it to a ball between her own. The man didn't know the meaning of the word. Heaven help the women in his life who expected more than the physical pleasure he took from them!

Glancing back at the still averted Bridget, she said stonily, 'I'm ready for the sale.'

Mockingly he stepped aside and let her precede him across the hall. 'The sun's hot, maybe you should find yourself a hat,' he suggested blandly as they reached the front door.

'I'll manage without,' she returned hotly, resenting every step of the way in his company as they traversed the gravelled track that led to the stretch of buildings, pens and corrals which were the ranch's lifeblood.

It was only later, when the sale was well under way and the sun beat unmercifully on her uncovered head, that Natalie regretted her stubbornness in not wearing a hat. Perched on the top rail of the sale area, she constantly had to lift her hand to shade her eyes as the parade of bulls went on. Reluctantly, she had to admit that Cal was an expert in his field. The select number of buyers were obviously aware of this, too, respecting him even when he held out for an original price. Blue Lake Ranch had always produced the finest bulls in the Valley, she reflected dreamily, as yet another broad-shouldered animal was brought prancing into the show ring. She could remember her father's excitement on sale day when his prize stock was paraded before shrewd buyers from near and far. Conscience smote her when she recalled how uninterested she had been in those sales—in the ranch as a whole. It was her father's domain, and he had never encouraged her interest.

But she had missed a lot of fun and excitement, she realised as her eyes strayed to the men lining the rails and saw the easy exchange of chitchat contrasted with the shrewd appraisal of Blue Lake's offerings. The lake itself, small and dark blue, shimmered in the distance. Swimming parties there had been a background to her growing up summers. Picnics on the narrow strand of beach at its south end had been fun times, her mother uncomplainingly providing sandwiches, cakes and soft drinks for the army of friends Natalie constantly invited. Jan, her bosom buddy, had always been there; Jason, Marie, Carl, Murray . . . oh yes, Murray had always been

there, however much his parents disapproved of
Natalie as a future wife for him. But Jan had been
there too, good solid Jan who would inherit good
solid ranchland.

Her eyes fell on Cal's tall lean figure as he bent to
secure the gate after the latest sale offering left the
pen, and she idly compared the two men. While
Murray had the strong well-set physique of the
Valley men, Cal had a racehorse leanness about him
that gave him an air of aristocracy, a fineness that
reached far back into the history of North America.
She couldn't imagine him as anything but what he
was, a man grown tough in the service of his calling.
Yet he could be physically tender; heat bathed her
face when she remembered the feel of his calloused
hands on the tenderest parts of her anatomy. Had
she truly imagined that they were Murray's hands
expertly moulding her body to the roused needs of
his?

Of course she had, she told herself disgustedly.
Murray was the only man who had stirred her in
that way, of course she had been thinking of him
while Cal Hendricks pawed her. She looked up as
the man she had been thinking about approached
from inside the corral. Reaching her, he put one foot
on the lowest rail and pushed his cowman's hat off
his forehead with one finger. As she looked down
from her perch his head lifted and their eyes met
with an impact that was almost physical. Natalie's
throat closed and her breath was trapped painfully
in her chest. No man had ever looked at her that
way before, his eyes burning into hers before they
dropped lazily to the soft outline of her mouth, rest-

ing there with indolent possession.

'Do I have your approval for the sales?' His tight-drawn mouth scarcely moved, yet he managed to inject a considerable amount of mockery into the few words.

'My—what?' she pulled herself up from the lethargy that had filled her limbs.

'Your approval. Didn't you say you came down here to supervise the sale?'

Natalie relaxed her hands on the top rail of the fence as life surged back into her. 'Everything seems in order,' she said stiffly, 'so you can complete the sales.'

'Thank you, ma'am.' With a completely ironic gesture he pulled his hat back down to shade his eyes and touched his fingers to the brim before turning abruptly away. The terse flatness of his shoulder muscles under his close-fitting beige shirt indicated more than words could have his irritation at having to consult a woman before completing the business details of the sale.

Her eyes lifted to the buyers who had now collected into small groups and she felt their curious eyes on her. Many of them she knew, men who ranched in the Valley or the surrounding area, and they were aware that, as Bridget had said, she didn't know one end of a bull from the other. But even the strangers eyed her curiously; in this man's world, none of them would have consulted the opinion of a stripling girl.

Instead of the surge of triumph she had expected, Natalie felt small, petty, vindictive. She hadn't meant to belittle Cal except on a personal basis, yet she had exposed him to the ridicule of his peers.

Without knowing quite what she did, she swung her legs over the top rail and jumped to the dusty earth, walking rapidly away from the huddled groups who were now more interested in details of pick-up and payment than in her small part in the sale. Her steps took her in the direction of the lake, and gradually, as bush growth gave way to sand, her thoughts coalesced into a pattern that made sense. So what if her actions had left Cal open to ridicule? He deserved everything that was coming to him. He had set himself up as arbiter of her movements, and that was something she had no need of. She was a grown woman, as wise as most in the ways of the world, she could direct her own life without help from the man her father had hired to run the ranch for him when he couldn't do it himself.

The beach opened suddenly, goldenly, before her as she stepped from bush trail to openness. Her eyes softened as they lit on the rounded expanse of blue water, the sweep of pines down to the farther shores bringing a translucent green to the shallower water. The sand was hot when she sat down and hugged her knees, her mind filled with the long-ago days that were happiest in her life. It had always seemed sunny like this then, the fierce burn of the sun's rays cooled effectively by an incisive dive off the wooden pier her father had constructed for just that purpose.

The pier had weathered, she noted, the yellow wood of earlier times having darkened to greyish brown, some of the boards sagging in places.

Her hand lifted to brush the hair back from her moist brow. It was hot, unusually hot for spring.

The lake, fed by streams that percolated down from the distant mountains, would be cold, but it looked inviting in its blueness. She glanced around at the bush-confined closeness of the small beach, though she knew that the lake, situated as it was well inside Forman property, held little possibility of invasion by strangers.

Rising, she undressed quickly and stepped naked on to the aged boards of the pier, her long slender feet avoiding the worst of the short planks as she walked to the end. For a moment she stood contemplating the blue rippled water, then, her arms forming an arrow of her body, she dived in.

Deadly cold stabbed at her, freezing her breath and numbing her limbs. Wildly, she struck out for deeper water, knowing it was even colder there but hoping the movement of her arms and legs would generate warmth to her limbs.

For a time it didn't, but then a curious kind of lethargy filled her and she floated easily on her back, her mind open to the memories that came rushing back. It seemed unlikely, but the sound of young voices calling to each other, laughing, screaming, were so real to her that she wished she had the energy to swim back and join in the beachside fun.

She longed for Murray's jet head to surface beside her, his hands to touch her in an intimate way he allowed only at the lake. He loved her, she knew, but it was as if he didn't trust the force of that love when they were alone. Then, he held himself in check, but at the lake it was different. Everybody played around there, frolicking around in near-nudity.

Then miraculously Murray came, his arm firm around her midriff, then brushing up over her breasts until it lodged across her shoulders, and she felt the rippling motion of the water on her limbs as he towed her to shore. But why was he taking her back there? Other people were there, people who would inhibit . . .

'Murray, don't!' she moaned. 'We can be alone out there.'

'We're alone here,' he said in a voice that grated uncharacteristically, and she realised as he drew her up to the hard-packed sand that it was too late anyway. Slowly, as his hands began to chafe life into her chilled limbs, the knowledge of what he had said penetrated the brain that oddly seemed as numb as her detached body.

Alone! It seemed years since she had been alone with Murray like this. Well, not quite like this, she acknowledged with a thrill of recognition as Murray's hands reached up over her hips with their half painful, half erotic movements. She had never imagined that his touch would be this demanding, this *forceful* . . . the gentleness she had always known had gone, and in its place was an undisguised maleness that sent shivers over her skin and deep tremors to the heart of her. Behind her closed lids she felt the vibrant return of warm blood coursing through her veins, and her arms reached up to the hard smooth damp male shoulders above her. Her exploring palms discovered the sparse covering of lean flesh, the rhythmic movement of sharply defined shoulder blades, the bare indentation of waist and . . . she drew a sharp breath of realisation . . . the absence of clothes of any sort.

'Oh, Murray,' she breathed, straining down on
the shoulders hovering over hers, 'kiss me, love me!'

The curse that shot against her eardrums was one
she had never heard Murray use, not even in his
most provoked moments, and her eyes flew open in
wide, flickering surprise. The man who had torn
himself from her grasping hold was standing beside
her, his arms rigidly at his sides, his expression
obscured by the slanting sunlight behind him. What
had she said, what had she done to make him spring
away from her as if her touch repelled him?

'Murray,' she faltered, 'what's wrong? I love you,
you must know that, and—I think you love me too.
Don't you?'

'Not being Murray, I wouldn't know about that,'
the rasping voice crashed against her ears. Lifting
her hand to shade her eyes, she gave an all too eloquent gasp.

'Oh, my God, *you*!' she whispered, the strength he
had recently chafed into her limbs fading rapidly
when it became totally clear that it was Cal, not
Murray, who stood condemningly over her.

'Me,' he confirmed without humour, turning aside
to pick up the clothes he had discarded before
coming to rescue her.

Rescue her! Dear God, why did it have to be him
of all people she had mistaken for Murray? Any other
man would have taken her ravings for what they
were, a meaningless castback to days that might have
been but had never been. A return to the security of
days that would never come again.

'Cal, I—I didn't know what I was saying.'

'Didn't you?' he asked harshly, turning back to her fully dressed, making her aware of her own nakedness so that she lifted belated hands to cover herself. Not that she needed to bother, she told herself with a trace of piqued tartness. The brown eyes were more impersonal than ever as they flicked over her inadequately shielded salient points. 'Maybe it's just as well that Murray Elson wasn't here then.'

Her lids fell, obscuring the speculative glow in her tawny eyes. What *would* have happened if it had been Murray, not Cal, chafing her numbed limbs back to life? Would she have permitted——? Would he have initiated——? By the time those tortuous questions had resolved themselves in her chaotic mind, Cal had gone, leaving the small strip of beach more desolate than she had ever known it.

Dressing quickly in the clothes she had abandoned so suddenly before plunging into the lake, Natalie nevertheless made no hasty retreat from the lake retreat. Instead, she dropped again to the sand and curved her arms around her knees as she stared out at the faintly rippled blue water.

Was she in love with Murray? From the events of the last half hour or so it would seem to be so. But he was married ... married to Jan, her best friend from kindergarten days. But those days were far behind. Could the loyalty of five-year-olds compare to the mature cravings of the sophisticated woman she had become? She had wanted the ultimate completion Murray—Cal—had set into motion with the intimacy of his touch minutes ago. Or was she wanton, craving any man's touch, even Cal's?

She wouldn't let herself believe that. It was

Murray she loved, Murray she had always loved. No city man had ever appealed to her for that reason. She was indissolubly tied to those sweet skeins of the past. And she would defy anyone, man or woman, to break those bonds that bound her.

Murray called her two days after the sale, his excuse for being in touch the birthday party he had planned for Jan.

'I thought you'd come up with something different,' he said, his voice husky at her ear, and Natalie melted at the intimacy implied in his seeking of help from her.

'Let's see,' she put her thought processes into action. 'How about—a fancy dress party, with everybody turning up in twenties clothes?'

'Everybody but Jan,' he returned drily. 'It has to be something she can join in without knowing she's joining in.'

Natalie frowned, concentrating. 'I know—why don't we have ordinary dress, but a belated Easter party where she'd have to search among the garden shrubs for her presents?'

'That sounds good,' Murray responded with less enthusiasm than she'd expected, though he sounded more eager as he went on, 'We could string lights through the trees and make nests in the branches for her gifts.'

'Yes,' she returned distantly, unsure of the emotions sweeping through her. Murray had to make some sort of concession to Jan's surprise birthday party, but did he have to sound this enthusiastic about it?

'Great! I'll tell everybody to make it small—what the hell, I'll tell them all what the idea is and they can bring suitably small presents.' Enthusiasm swelled in the gathering excitement of his tone, and Natalie felt her fingers grow stiff around the receiver. How could he sound this enthralled at the prospect of surprising plain old Jan? How, when he knew as well as she did that an invisible bond melded them together as indivisibly as the stars were attracted to the orbit of the moon?

'What about the food?' she asked coolly, struggling against the griping pangs of jealousy that crept insiduously into the softest part of her.

'Jean can see to that,' he told her confidently. 'She's coming back next week, and she'd never forgive me if I didn't let her in on the party for Jan.'

'Oh, good.' Nothing in Natalie's collected tones indicated the force of the fires raging within her. How could Murray be expected to know that she herself had been planning the buffet style meal where the guests would help themselves to asparagus tips dredged in lemon butter, tiny *vol-au-vents* filled with chicken, beef or salmon in a piquant sauce, a dessert of grapes halved and pressed into layers of cream cheese and pears in the form of a huge bunch of grapes? Murray was being tactful, considerate of the woman who produced the bulk of Ridgewood's meals.

'That's fine,' Murray said with surprising formality into her attentive ear, and she surmised that someone else had come into the room he was phoning from. 'I appreciate your help in this matter.'

'You're entirely welcome,' she responded sweetly,

dropping her own voice to a similarly intimate
cadence. 'Just let me know when you need me.'

'You can bet on that,' Murray said huskily, his
voice seeming to be dredged from some deep inborn
politeness when he added, 'I'll get in touch with you
very soon.'

Natalie stared for long moments at the receiver
she had returned to its cradle long after the conversation was concluded. She couldn't have imagined
that husky intimacy, that indisputable awareness of
all that had been between them once . . . could she?

No, she told herself confidently as she left the hall
and walked mindlessly towards the safe haven of her
room. Murray was as conscious of that tie that bound
them as much as she . . . hadn't it been obvious in
the deepened cadences of his tone, the intimacy
implied when his voice had dropped to husky assurance as soon as someone else had entered the room
he had phoned from?

God, she thought with sudden weariness as she
fell on the bed that had been hers for countless years,
Love had its own depths of hell, its own tortuous
questions and its own twisted answers. Was love this
yearning she had for a man who had figured prom-
inently in her youth? A man married to no less than
her girlhood confidant, Jan of the calm steadiness
who had been as close as—closer?—than a sister.
Embarrassment burned now on her fevered skin as
Natalie recalled the soul-baring confessions she had
indulged in with stoic Jan. How she loved Murray,
but worried about his lack of true ardour. Her breath
caught on the implications of that thought. Had she
really believed, way back then, that Murray lacked

the necessary fervour of a man in love?

But what had she known about it then? Honesty compelled her to admit that Murray's kisses had inspired no more than the beginning stir of a desire that had come to fruition only under Cal's expert tutelage.

Cal . . . was it really possible to learn about love—no, she corrected mentally, physical passion—from a man you hated? She supposed that might be so, if the man was Cal Hendricks. Speculation about his past was useless, unnecessary . . . she didn't need a detailed history to know that he was as experienced with women as he was in ranch affairs. In neither area was he a novice, and that conclusion led her to seek others. What had brought him to the Valley? He was surely a man used to giving orders, not taking them, so what had disrupted his life before Doug Forman had hired him as ranch manager? The answer was most likely in the other area of his expertise . . . a woman.

Natalie stared thoughtfully at the pristine whiteness of the ceiling. What kind of a woman would inspire that kind of love in a man like Cal? A beautiful one, probably. Despite his lack of formally handsome features, he had a basic male attraction few women would resist. Had she been married, this woman he had cared for?

The thought was enough to send her abruptly into an upright position on the bed. Was that why Cal was so alert to her own feelings for Murray? He had denied himself, so why shouldn't she join in his misery?

Yes, that sounded like Cal, hard and strong and

immovable, and he expected her to be the same way.
One certainty after another leapt into her mind.
Cal's soured romance was his business; just as her
feelings for Murray were hers. He liked Jan, was
concerned about her happiness, but he knew nothing
about what had gone before. Jan had stabbed her in
the back—she had admitted as much that day she
had come to lunch. Murray had always been hers,
Natalie's, and her so-called friend had slipped in at
a vulnerable time in their relationship and made off
with the spoils—helped, she reflected acidly, by her
family's rich ranch land.

If Murray had been weak it was in the area of not
having the inner fortitude to defy his parents and
marry the girl he loved, not the one who had the
most to offer in a worldly sense.

And he did love her, Natalie—still loved her in
spite of three years of marriage to sweetly placid
Jan. He had been about to tell her that, she was
sure, when Cal had interrupted them on the porch
at Ridgewood. Why couldn't he mind his own
business and brood on his own lost love without
applying his moralistic standards to others? Maybe
it was time Mr Cal Hendricks faced the fact that
he couldn't manipulate others into his own way of
thinking.

With that thought in mind, she said brightly at
the dinner shared with Cal and Bridget, 'I'll be
spending quite a lot of time at Ridgewood for the
next little while. It's a secret, so I can't tell you just
why I'll be there.'

Cal's eyes swivelled hardly round on her, their flat
brown uncompromising in their appraisal. 'It doesn't

need too much imagination to guess what the secret is,' he stated cryptically, his mouth closing like a trap over the words.

'Oh, now, Cal,' Bridget reprimanded gently before turning with a smile to Natalie. 'Are you and Jan planning something? I remember when you were young . . .'

The phone in the hall jangled an interruption to her words and she got up from the table with a resigned sigh and went from the kitchen muttering imprecations on people who called when decent folks were sitting down to their meal.

'You're not going to Ridgewood because you've planned something with Jan, are you?' Cal stated flatly as soon as the housekeeper's robust figure had disappeared.

Natalie looked at him, the dancing lights in her eyes reflecting the deep pleasure she felt in knowing that she had needled him, obviously worried him.

'Not with Jan, no,' she confirmed, taking up her napkin to dab a non-existent spot beside her mouth. 'Murray and I have some—business to settle that doesn't concern Jan. Well,' she considered, looking thoughtful as she replaced her napkin on her lap and poised her fork over her portion of Bridget's succulent beef pie, 'it's something that concerns Jan, but not directly, if you know what I mean.'

'I know what you mean,' he grated with a fury that startled her momentarily. 'Now you just listen to me——'

'No!' she snapped, replacing her fork with a clatter, her eyes snapping venom as they looked fearlessly into his, 'you listen to me. My life is my own business.

It has nothing, repeat *nothing* , whatsoever to do with you. Things happened in this Valley long before you ever heard of it. Things that concern me and—other people. It's not your business, can't you understand that? Why don't you concentrate on your own problems? What was she like, Cal,' she mocked with feline pleasure, 'your unreachable woman?'

'My *what*?' he ejaculated, his face whitening under his leathered tan features, and Natalie experienced a surge of triumph at the rightness of her diagnosis of his ills.

'Oh, dear,' Bridget worried as she came back from the telephone, seeming not to sense the tension between the two as she seated herself opposite Cal. 'Poor Jan!'

'Jan?'

'*Jan*?'

Natalie gave Cal a half irritated, half abstracted glance when his question coincided with her own, then she turned her attention back to Bridget.

'Murray's mother is ill—you know his parents moved to Kamloops when Murray married and took over the ranch?' she added in an aside to Natalie. 'Well, it seems Clara Elson's had to take to her bed again, and she wants Jan to come and be with her for a while. She's very fond of her, always has been, she was pleased when Murray married Jan.'

'Who was on the phone?' Natalie interrupted the discourse tersely.

'It was Murray. He wanted to talk to you, but I said you were eating——'

'You had no right to do that!' Natalie fumed, bunching up her napkin and throwing it petulantly at the side of her plate. If Murray had wanted to speak to her, it could only be to tell her that with Jan gone they would have a breathing space to talk about what was closest to both their hearts. And now Bridget had interfered, implying that Natalie was too busy eating to listen to that vitally important message. She was on her feet and near the door when Bridget's politely withdrawn voice, the one she used when she was offended to the quick, stopped her precipitate flight in the direction of the phone.

'It's no good calling Murray back, he was just leaving for a cattlemen's meeting at the community hall.'

Natalie teetered uncertainly between chancing a call that might find Murray still at Ridgewood, or on the other hand be answered by Jan or Jean McLeod. She wanted to speak to neither of those, only to Murray. Murray whose first thought had been to call her.

'So you'll have all the time in the world for your secret assignations at Ridgewood,' Cal remarked drily, leaning back from his cleared plate but not looking round at Natalie.

'Yes, I will, won't I?' she addressed the back of his head, her voice sweetly venomous. Her eyes lifted then to Bridget, who had risen to clear the plates, her folded jowls ominous in their tightness. 'Bridget, I'm sorry, I didn't mean to upset you. It was just that—well, I'd rather have talked to Murray myself. There are things we—have to discuss.'

'Surely,' the housekeeper said in her most dignified voice, stiff disapproval in her rounded figure as she went to deposit the used plates on the sink counter.

'But I'm thinking you'll wait now until his wife comes back.'

'But why should I? What Murray and I are planning has nothing to do with Jan.'

Bridget sniffed her disbelief while Cal looked on with his flatly inexpressive eyes. Natalie had come back to the table, though she stood behind her chair rather than sinking into it. It was typical of Bridget to treat her still as the child she had nurtured long ago.

'A man's business is always his wife's concern,' she intoned now in the teaching voice she had used then, adding, 'especially when his business is with another woman.'

'Oh, for heaven's sake, Bridget,' Natalie burst out impatiently, 'all Murray and I are doing is planning a birthday party for Jan! What's so bad about that?'

Bridget turned from the dessert pie she was slicing and looked at Natalie with relief in her button eyes. 'A birthday party,' she echoed. 'Is that all?'

'Of course it's all,' she snapped. 'What did you think? That I was planning to spirit Murray away from Jan while her back was turned?' She wouldn't do that, she told herself furiously, and silently. If and when she and Murray decided to be together as destiny had meant them to be, Jan would be the first to know. But now wasn't the right time to tell Bridget that . . . one enemy in the camp was enough. Her eyes slid across to Cal's closed expression. What was he thinking? For some strange reason that seemed to matter, though she couldn't for the life of her think why. His opinions didn't matter to her one way or the other, now that she knew her surmise about another woman were correct. No man completely innocent could have looked as Cal had at her shot in the dark.

'Something like that,' he startled her by injecting into the conversation, 'but then you're aware that Murray Elson would no more break up his comfortable marriage with a land-rich wife than he would have gone against his parents' wishes three years ago when he married her. It's all a question of supply and demand,' he ended on a drawl that sent Natalie's nerves into a furious jangle.

'Blue Lake Ranch wasn't far behind Jan's family property,' she gritted, 'as you'll know from the price the new owners have pledged for it. And I've no doubt you know that,' she added with sweet savagery, 'just as you know a lot of things that are none of your business!'

'This ranch has increased in value, like everything else, over the past three years,' he acknowledged with a terse nod, 'but it never has and never will equal the value of Elson and Stanton property joined into one. Unfortunately for you,' his eyes appraised her with cool insolence, 'your childhood sweetheart settled for land and a wife who wouldn't rock his fragile boat.'

'Nothing about Murray is fragile,' she told him stonily as Bridget placed hearty wedges of pie at each place and returned with the bowl of whipped cream that inevitably accompanied it. 'I'm not hungry, Bridget,' she said with lofty detachment, refusing the pie which, in truth, sent her taste buds into ecstasy. Nothing would induce her to sit at the table in company with a man who made a virtue of virtue. He had all the answers, except the ones that were most important in a personal sense. Love had escaped both of them in similar ways, but there the sameness ended. Where Cal had given up, she would fight to the end to right the wrongs life had dealt out to her.

Ignoring Bridget's renewed reproach, evident in the faded light of her snapping dark eyes, Natalie stalked from the kitchen and paused in front of the telephone, mutely inviting in the front hall. By now Murray would have left for his meeting, so there was no useful purpose to be served by dialling the Ridgewood number now. And why would she bother with an impersonal instrument? she wondered as she continued on to the bedroom where she spent such a lot of her time these days.

She would ride over to Ridgewood in the morning—or maybe at the lunch hour when Murray would perhaps be at home. They would talk quietly, sanely, discussing the problem that was uppermost in both their minds. Love, in its true sense, had nothing to do with land and its acquisition through marriage. Murray had been dominated by his parents, too willing to give in to their incessant naggings about making a suitable marriage. He was master now at Ridgewood. She had seen, and loved, the new maturity about him, the steely will that had developed over the past three years. Murray was his own man now, free to choose the wife who would bring him the assets Jan had never possessed—beauty, wit, a flair for decorative ambience and social awareness. Oh, yes, Murray had finally broken out of the cocoon of parental pressure and become a man in his own right.

CHAPTER SIX

RIDGEWOOD drowsed under an unusually hot spring sun as Natalie cantered up to the hedge-enclosed driveway. Rounding the last curve of the drive, she reined in Josh, one of the more venerable members of the Blue Lake stables, and stared breathlessly at the weathered lineaments of the house she had been in awe of all her life.

The gardens stretching in new-budded greenness in front of the house were the love-child of Murray's mother, the indomitable Clara who had concealed beneath her thorny exterior this penchant for beauty, the carving of lawns and flower beds from prairie wilderness. Early Elsons had confined their estate-building instincts to the construction of the turreted mansion that dominated the scenery for miles around. It had been left to future generations, in the form of Clara, to tame the dusty soil into lawns and flower beds.

Jan must have taken over where the old lady left off, Natalie reflected drily, her tawny eyes sweeping the neat black soil beds with their newly installed seedlings which would become a blaze of colour as time went on. None of the men involved in ranch work had time for fussing with prettiness; that was woman's domain, and women like Jan accepted it.

Urging Josh up to the gravelled forecourt of the house, Natalie slid from his back and tethered him to the rail enclosing a spring green paddock. As he

nosed interestedly at the succulent grass escaping
from under the fence, she went towards the house,
her heels crunching the chipped gravel. She noticed
things now that she had missed when she and Cal
had come here to dinner. The house, despite its age,
sported new paint on its elaborately pillared porch,
and windows exposed to the sun glittered their
sparkling cleanliness. Red brick porch enamel contrasted starkly with the white of wrought iron casual
furniture set in orderly fashion along its length.

A pang that was painful struck Natalie in her
middle as she raised her hand to the big brass lion's
head that took the place of the city's electric buzzer.
All this should have been hers . . . not Jan's . . . never
Jan's. This house demanded the panache she could
have brought to it; parties given to celebrate the
rising of a harvest moon, or the native Indian rejoic-
ing in the lifegiving forces of the sun—any excuse
would have been enough for her to stage a party, to
make Murray proud of her, of his heritage.

She was still lost in the fantasy of what might have
been when the door was opened widely and Jean
McLeod's round-cheeked face looked at her enquiringly.

'Hello, Miss Forman, I heard you were back in
town.'

'Yes. Is——?'

'I'm really sorry about your father,' the Elson
housekeeper pursued, her blue eyes sincerely regretful as they took in Natalie's hip-moulding beige
slacks and brown checked shirt. 'He was a good man
and he'll be missed in the Valley.'

'Thanks, Jean. I came to see——'

'Mrs Elson isn't here,' Jean told her regretfully, her hand firmly protecting the door as if she expected Natalie to storm the house. 'She had to go to——'

'I know,' Natalie dismissed the news brusquely, stepping into the cool widths of the hall and turning impatiently to the bewildered housekeeper. 'I came to see Mr Elson—are you expecting him home?'

Jean stared at her perplexedly, and Natalie could almost hear the machinations of her brain. A Valley girl, she knew that Murray Elson and Natalie Forman had been a thing at one time, that she had disappeared just before his marriage to Jan.

'Well, I——' she hesitated, 'he—sometimes comes in for lunch, but more often than not he——'

'I'll wait,' Natalie brushed aside the stammering objections and went with sure feet to the far side of the hall where she paused outside the door that led to Murray's inner sanctum, the place where he conducted ranch business. 'Let him know I'm here when he comes in, will you?'

Jean's tightlipped nod affected her not at all as she turned the door handle and went in to the room that was solely Murray's. Had she chosen this because it held no traces of Jan? Maybe so, she reflected as she stepped with her racehorse grace to the centre of the room and looked around her.

Everything spoke of Murray, from the solid dark wood of the desk to the library shelves lining one wall filled with ranching manuals and records of Ridgewood reaching back into the dim reality of previous Elsons who had farmed this land. Hardy people, men and women who were not afraid of the hard work entailed in the breaking of virgin land.

Murray had inherited at least some of that fortitude. Some, not all. Would his male ancestor have been as ready as Murray to sacrifice true love for the expediency of marrying for land gain?

Yes, probably he would have, she told herself with wry honesty as she walked to the twin windows overlooking the rear of Ridgewood, the working area of the ranch visible through the shelter belt of trees to her left.

But Murray wasn't like that. He was a product of the present generation, the one which scorned the accumulation of land through a loveless marriage. A man made it on his own or not at all. Yet—Murray had married Jan, who had only her family property to recommend her. It was . . .

'Nat?'

She swung round, her head still filled with what might have been, what should have been, and saw Murray framed in the open doorway, lines of fatigue running from nose to mouth slightly marring the dark good looks she had admired for so long.

'Oh, Murray,' she said, flustered. 'I hoped you'd come home for lunch today. I—needed to talk to you.'

'Really?' His booted spurs jangled as he walked towards her, a haunted look in his eyes making her lift her hands in a half placating gesture. 'It's good of you to still be thinking of Jan's birthday party, but she's not going to be here to celebrate it. Didn't Bridget give you my message last night?'

'Yes, of course she did,' Natalie responded sharply, chilled by his matter-of-fact manner. 'But she'll probably be back in time for her birthday celebrations, won't she?'

Her eyes clung to the dark circles of his, hating her dependency yet knowing that this man held the key to her love life. Her gaze held to the rounded line of his jaw, the warm mobility of his well-shaped mouth.

'Yes, but——' He looked at her, a strange kind of anguish in his eyes. It was as if he had dipped into the hell she herself had known since his engagement to Jan had been announced.

'Murray,' she breathed, her feet winged as they took her to stand in front of him, 'it doesn't really matter about Jan or—anybody. We love each other, nothing else matters.' Her hands went in a frenzy of need to the taut muscles in his upper arms and slid up to the hard apex of his neck, her fingers probing lovingly between the silky dark hairs there. 'I love you, Murray,' she breathed, her mouth moist as it lifted to the firmly held outline of his. She felt the heavy warmth of his hands lift to enfold her, to streak searchingly over the brown check of her shirt, warming her flesh with the heat of his. 'Oh, Murray . . . darling!'

An ecstasy wilder than anything she had ever known flowed through her when Murray's mouth fastened on hers, his mouth almost desperate as it probed and sought the inner essence she offered so freely. He loved her . . . Murray loved her!

'Darling, we'll be together for always,' she murmured feverishly against the warmth of his mouth, 'forget all that's happened in between. We were foolish, stupid to let a little argument come between us. Oh, Murray!' she rained quick kisses on the area round his mouth, her eyes still shining with an emotional glow when Murray put her abruptly from him.

'Murray?' she whispered, feeling her heart turn over then begin to hammer in her chest. His eyes stared bleakly down into hers, and there was something—shame?—far back in their depths. 'What's wrong, Murray? You know we still love each other, why are you looking at me like that?'

Murray shook his head impatiently, as if brushing away an irritating fly. 'We're not in love, Nat, I'm not sure we ever were.'

'What are you saying?' she cried incredulously. 'We've been in love since we were children! Everybody in the Valley knew that we——'

'Everybody knew that we went through a form of puppy love,' he corrected harshly, dropping his hands from the tops of her arms and moving stiffly across to stand with his back to the desk. 'That's all it was, Nat, puppy love. And like puppies, we played and fought and made up again. Real love is something different, something you and I never had. It's giving, and sharing, and working to make each other happy.'

'How very nice,' she jeered from somewhere inside the shock numbing her senses, 'and how very dull!'

Murray's shoulders lifted in a shrug, and incredibly a faint smile touched the mouth that still bore the traces of hers. 'That's what I always knew about you, Nat. The kind of life I would have offered you would never have been enough for you. You'd be hard for any man to handle; for me, you'd have been impossible.'

She stared at him as if seeing him for the first time. Had he really known all this way back, then? Her brain reached into her memory file, back to the time of their most intimate moments together. She had always depended on Murray, she realised, to call a halt to deeper involvement; it was Murray who had drawn back when she would have gone forward. She had thought he was exerting a will-power she herself possessed in small measure. Now—was it possible that what he was implying was true? That he had been—*afraid* of her?

'No,' she denied aloud, 'you married Jan instead of me because of her family's land! Can you deny that was a factor?'

His jaw hardened, and he acknowledged through tight lips, 'It didn't hurt, but,' he went on quietly when triumph flared in Natalie's eyes, 'it wouldn't have mattered if she'd had nothing. I was in love with Jan when I married her . . . I'm in love with her now.'

Hurt seared behind Natalie's breastbone and she resorted again to mockery. 'If you're so much in love with her, how come you were kissing me like a parched man at a well, a minute ago?'

Murray's skin seemed to pale under his tan, and he straightened from his half-sitting position against the desk. 'I'm not proud of that,' he said softly. 'You're an attractive woman, even more so than when you were a girl, and I'm no eunuch. You offered yourself, and I was taken by surprise.'

Her breath drew in on an indignant hiss. '*I* offered myself? Don't insult me! I don't have to throw myself at weak-kneed prairie hicks! There are plenty of men in the city who'd——'

'I know that, Nat,' he interrupted with a remote earnestness that chilled her. 'Look, you'll be going away from here soon, and you're going to be a pretty rich girl when you do. There's going to be lots of men who can give you what I never can—love, marriage, children.'

Ignoring the spasm of pain that crossed his face at the last mention, Natalie cried wildly, 'I'm not like Jan! I don't need to *buy* a husband!'

'Neither did Jan,' he retorted with controlled calm.

'Didn't she?' Natalie scorned, and spun on her heel to walk to the door, turning there to rake him with blazing eyes. 'Maybe you've talked yourself into believing that you married Jan for love, but you'll never convince me of that!'

'I don't have to convince you of anything,' Murray said with such indisputable logic that she clenched her teeth and threw open the door, marching across the hall and out of the house in a blind state of fury.

Impatient when Josh was slowly reluctant to leave his grazing area, she untied him from the rail and pulled jerkily on the rains to gain his attention before swinging lithely into the saddle and setting off down the shaded driveway. Anger thumped its heavy beat at her heart, and she stared unseeingly ahead as Josh pursued his steady gait.

Damn Murray Elson, she fumed in cold fury . . . damn all men and their scheming minds! In half a dozen words Murray had negated everything that had been between them, made nonsense of the love she had cherished all this time. She had loved him, she did love him ... she *must* love him. Without Murray to concentrate her emotions on she would just be one aching void, a woman without focus. He had filled her life for so long, she couldn't imagine an existence without him.

She guided Josh with automatic precision to the prairie land that led to Blue Lake, her mind a seething churn of conflicting emotions. She loved Murray ... she hated Murray. The seesaw bent first one way, then the other. How could she hate him if she loved him?

They drew up and paused on the knoll looking down at Blue Lake Ranch with its sparkling lake reflecting a blue sheen. Its inviting calmness reminded her of Cal Hendricks and the way he had rescued her from its cold depths. Without conscious volition, she compared the two men. Murray who had been unable to resist the chance to make love to her; Cal who had chafed her naked limbs without taking advantage of her vulnerability. Strange ... she would have sworn that the events would have had diametrically opposite results. Cal, she knew, was far from the eunuch Murray had mentioned in connection with himself. The two times he had kissed her proved that beyond doubt. Yet he had made no attempt to make love to her, there on the secluded beach.

She felt a warm wetness on her cheeks as Josh started downhill, and her hand lifted to wipe them irritatedly away. What did she care if Cal found her unattractive? He didn't matter in her scheme of things. Only Murray mattered ... yes, she ack-

nowledged wryly with a loud sniff that no one but
she and Josh heard, she still loved him.

In the hollow where new-sprung wildflowers
opened their yellow, gold, crimson petals, she pulled
Josh to a halt and slid down from the saddle, giving
the horse his delighted head and throwing herself to
the sweet-smelling grass while he began to browse in
that horse paradise.

She stared up at the sky, the earth faintly damp
under her. Cottony clouds drifted lazily across the
sun in the higher draughts, but they obscured little
of the noon sun's heat. Heady scents filled her nostrils; the basic dampness of the earth under her, the
delicate perfume of the wildflowers dotted thickly in
the grass. How she loved this country! Nothing in
the city could compare with it.

Yet . . . she felt the warm well of tears again when
she remembered that in a mere matter of months
the city would be her habitat. The world would be
her oyster when the new owners of Blue Lake Ranch
made their payment. She would be able to live
wherever she liked in the life-style of her choosing.

Why, then, she asked herself agonisedly, did she
want nothing more than to live here in the the land
of her fathers, growing old in the country she knew,
that knew her? Oh, Murray . . . Murray!

So caught up was she in the intoxication of her
surroundings that she failed to hear the swift beat of
hooves across the meadow, the whisper of grass under
boots when Cal came to stand over her. Swiftly, she
raised a hand to brush away the tears that had cooled
on her cheeks and she looked defiantly up at his
whip-lean figure as it stood over her.

'You're crying,' he stated the obvious, the flat brown of his eyes touching on the moisture streaking her cheeks, the new-washed clarity of her tawny eyes.

'You don't say,' she mocked, pulling herself into a sitting position and sliding her arms down in a defensive gesture over her knees. 'Isn't that a woman's privilege?'

Cal pushed off the hat that shaded his face and dropped it on the grass as he sat beside her. 'Even women don't cry without a reason,' he shrugged. His eyes narrowed as he levelled them on the pure line of her profile, exposed by the style that drew her hair back in a bunch at her nape. 'Where have you been?'

Natalie dragged her eyes away from the distant smudge of blue mountains and stared frostily at him. 'Why should I have been anywhere particular?'

His head swivelled to take in their idyllic surroundings. 'There's nothing here that would be a cause for the waterworks to start flowing, especially in a woman like you.' He turned back to face her, the derisive smile flickering round his tightly held lips stirring her into a fury that went far beyond what circumstances demanded.

'What do you mean, a woman like me?' she flashed heatedly. 'You know nothing about what kind of woman I am! You're so typical of the men around here—you think because I spent a few years in the city I'm some kind of Jezebel! Well, you're mistaken, Mr Cal Hendricks—not that I care what you think of me, but I was brought up to respect myself and I lost my job because I wouldn't——'

She broke off and bit her lip furiously. Why had she said such a thing to Cal Hendricks? It would amuse him, with his casually experienced approach to sex, to know that she had run away like a scalded cat from that kind of involvement.

But his voice had an unexpectedly gentle note when he put his hand over hers and stopped her shredding destruction of the plump grass between them. 'So that's why you're not in any hurry to get back there? I wondered. When I said "a woman like you",' he went on with maddening reasonableness, 'I meant that you're not the kind to cry for little reason, it would have to be something big. Want to tell me about it?'

He hadn't released her hand, but Natalie made no effort to pull it out from under. Although she couldn't stand him, there was something comforting about the way his warm flesh totally protected hers.

'I—I was just feeling sorry for myself because I—have to leave here soon,' she faltered, knowing that she spoke no lie as her eyes wandered to the front again to see the perfection around them. There was no reason for Cal to know the absolute truth, that Murray had shattered every dream she had ever cherished, making a mockery of their love. She started and blinked up into Cal's face when he spoke harshly.

'I also thought you were the kind of woman who wouldn't find it necessary to lie,' he gritted, hurting her knuckles as his hand closed on hers. 'You saw Murray Elson a while ago, didn't you?'

Natalie drew a deep, quavering breath, but her eyes were steady on his when she said coldly, 'I saw

Murray, yes. And you don't have to worry any more about me splitting up that marriage. That was your concern, wasn't it?' she questioned with a calmness that equalled his. 'At this moment, I don't know who I hate the most—Murray, or myself for being such a fool as to——'

'We're all fools sometimes,' he interrupted as if he didn't want to hear the rest of what she was saying, 'but not many of us have the courage to admit it.'

'I can't imagine you ever admitting such a thing,' she scorned as she finally pulled her hand from his grip and stared blindly at the grass patterns embedded in her palm. 'Anyway, whatever you think, I was saying goodbye to the Valley when you came. There's nothing here for me now.'

'You don't have to say goodbye to it,' Cal said so quietly that she jerked her face round to his and stared at him, puzzled.

'Of course I do. There's nothing here to hold me now.' Her parents were gone, Bridget was ageing, Murray was—a part of her past that she would have to put behind her in a place far from here.

'No,' Cal shook his head and met the half question in her eyes. 'You could marry me,' he said quietly.

Natalie stared incredulously into the eyes that were only slightly darker than her own. One emotion after another chased across her expressive features; shock gave way to disbelief, which was in turn chased away by an absurd urge to laugh. Something about Cal's seriously set expression stemmed the last, but she felt a wave of hysteria still rising in her when she gasped.

'Marry *you*? *Marry* you?' The sky whirled around his thick brown hair as she tried to focus on the features that were far from the perfection she would have demanded in a husband. 'You're joking!'

'A man's first proposal of marriage isn't a joking matter.'

Natalie's eyes widened as it sank into her brain that he was deadly serious. Unromantically serious. What reason other than romance would a man have for proposing marriage to a girl who was virtually a stranger to him? Murray's words came back to haunt her. Lots of men would want to marry her when the ranch sale went through! What wouldn't an itinerant worker like Cal give to lay his hands on that kind of wealth!

'Why me?' she played for time.

'I need a wife, you need a husband.'

This couldn't be happening, she told herself even as she asked, 'Just like that? Don't you have to feel something for each other—like love? I don't even like you!'

The insult passed harmlessly over his confidently set head. 'We get along well enough in the most important area,' he said with a significance that brought bright colour to her cheeks. 'The rest will follow from that.'

'You're just unreal!' The humour that had threatened just below the surface now erupted in violent spasms of unconcealed laughter. 'You're—like somebody from—a Victorian—novel,' she gasped, her hand lifting to wipe the different quality of tears from her eyes. 'Oh, Cal, people these days get married because they—because they *love* each other, not because it's convenient to have a wife or a husband.'

She sobered abruptly when his hand reached up to curve round her nape under the heavy fall of her hair, his fingers pressing with sure insistence to angle her face up to his. He said nothing, but she saw his intent in the fierce glitter that lit the surface of his normally flat brown eyes. The same trick of light or whatever it was that made him appear devastatingly attractive at close quarters sprang into being and she murmured a defensive 'No, Cal!' when the taut steel of his arms surrounded her and pulled her back, back to the moist embrace of earth and grass and flowers.

His rough fingers traced a path over her smooth skin from temple to mouth and his lips followed lightly along it. She felt like a prairie creature caught into frozen immobility by the bright glare of truck headlights, her eyes wide open in almost somnambulistic torpor as she felt Cal's mouth on her skin, his hair falling forward on to her brow as he teased with deadly intent the sensitive line of her jaw, the area surrounding her mouth.

Why didn't he kiss her properly? something screamed inside her, and her head shifted a fraction so that her lips met and fused with the tormenting thrust of his. Her senses swam and were lost in the sea of sensation that flooded her and drowned out every scruple she had ever known. The world she had been so acutely aware of moments before faded into obscurity. There was only this man and her own timeless need for the fulfilment he offered. Her hands lifted and slid across the hard back of his shoulder muscles before lodging in the thick dampness of hair at his nape.

Everything she had known before rushed away and was held in a state of suspended animation. She had never been this intimate with a man before, yet she knew as he levered the hard lines of his body over her that he desired her in the way a man wants a woman. And she . . . she wanted him in that same way, wanted the hard caress of his fingers at the alerted peaks of her breasts, the seeking thrust of his maleness against her . . . not even Murray had raised her to this pitch . . .

Murray! Murray who had told her a scant hour ago that he loved Jan, not her.

'You see?' Cal rasped at her ear, his breath coming in heavy snatches. 'We're not so mismatched, are we?'

Mismatched . . . no, in a physical way they were perfectly attuned. But shouldn't there be more than the physical in a relationship as all encompassing as marriage? What she had said was true. She didn't even like Cal as a person, yet her every impulse was to yield to him, to take from him the same satisfaction he demanded of her.

'Cal, I——' She felt the sag of withdrawal in her body and knew that he felt it too. 'I can't marry you just because I—I want you to make love to me. There's more than that, can't you see? There *has* to be more than that!' she ended despairingly. 'People don't get married because they're—good in bed. They have to like each other as persons, too!'

He sat up, away from her, the harsh lines falling into place beside his mouth and eyes as if they had never been erased. 'There's enough basis for marriage between us as far as I'm concerned,' he said with blunt certitude. 'One thing leads to another. Liking can lead to loving, loving can lead to liking. There's no rule-book that says it has to be one or the other.'

Natalie sat up above him as her fingers closed the buttons on her brown and white checked shirt over the swollen curves of her breasts. There was something ridiculous, unbelievable, about sitting here in a flower-bedecked meadow talking about a union of two people as if it were a business proposition. Business—wasn't that what was behind Cal's proposal of marriage? Doug Forman's daughter was a catch in any man's eyes, particularly to a man with as few means of support as Cal Hendricks. Did he really think that she was easy prey just because he had used his male expertise on her? Venom rose acidly to her throat, replacing the molten glow of moments ago through her veins.

'Do you really think I'm so desperate for a man that I'd let him marry me for the money I have coming to me from my father's property?' she scorned, anger lending impetus to her upward thrust to a standing position.

'I'm not interested in your money,' Cal said flatly as he rose and topped her height by several inches. 'In fact, I'd make a condition that what you have you keep. I've no need for a woman to support me.'

'No?' she enquired, sweetly acid as she lodged her hands on her hips and glared up at him. 'You think I'd be content to follow you around the country to wherever you can find a job?'

'I won't be moving,' he returned evenly, his hands moving in a brushing gesture over the hips of his taut blue jeans. 'I'll be making my home in the Valley.'

'Really?' Natalie mocked, resisting an impulse to follow his example and rid herself of the clinging grass she knew must decorate her back. 'And just where had you planned on settling? There isn't a property available within thirty miles, and no one I know of needs a hired hand right now.'

'I've no intention of working as a hired hand,' he retorted quietly. 'In a few months' time, Blue Lake Ranch and everything connected with it will be mine.'

CHAPTER SEVEN

NATALIE'S fingers curved convulsively round the
waistband of her jeans as she stared in open-mouthed
amazement at Cal. A strand of his thick brown hair
lifted in the breeze soughing gently up the Valley,
then fell back on his rugged forehead, giving him a
younger look. Yet there was still the deep mark of
maturity round his mouth and eyes, in the decisive
clench of his jaw.

'What did you say?' she whispered drily, her hand
rising automatically to brush at a fly buzzing threa-
teningly near. She couldn't have heard him correctly
. . . or else this was her day for receiving a lifetime
store of surprises! Her emotions had swung from one
absurd level to another, leaving her with a sickness at
the pit of her stomach. How could she take in now
that Cal—*Cal?*—was the new owner of Blue Lake?
Her bewilderment was reflected in the dulled yellow
brown of her eyes, and she subsided weakly back to
her former position on the grass without question
when Cal indicated that she should do so.

'I'm sorry, Natalie, it wasn't my intention to tell
you like this with no preliminaries,' he said in perfunctory apology, 'but when a man asks a woman to
marry him she has the right to know what kind of
life he can offer her, what kind of background he's
from.'

Natalie's head lifted and she squinted at him, her brow furrowing between her eyes. 'I don't know anything about your background,' she said in a cutting voice that indicated her indifference to that fact. 'You could be married, widowed, divorced, whatever. It really doesn't concern me, because I've no intention of marrying you now or at any future time.'

Cal seemed to note the irritated rub of her hand at the back of her neck, stiffened by staring up at him, and he dropped to her side. Not at all put out by her ill temper, he said, 'But aren't you curious about how I came to own your father's ranch?'

'That could bear a little explaining,' she returned acidly, surveying him with frosty precision as he took up a more comfortable position beside her, his long form stretched easily on the turf, his elbows propping up the upper half of his body. She felt no compunction about turning him down out of hand, but she was nevertheless aware that he had the smooth-muscled attraction of an animal of prey. An animal that lay in thickets and pounced when his victim least expected it. Natalie passed a wiping hand over her damp brow. What kind of thoughts were those? Judging from the cool, collected expression on Cal's face, her rejection of his surprise proposal hadn't bothered him one bit.

'I owned property south of here, near the States' border,' he began his explanation unhurriedly. 'It was a sizeable ranch, left to me by my father when he died ten years ago. About six months before I came up here, the government in its wisdom decided to build a hydro-electric dam in my area and they gave me a year to re-locate. Paying me, incidentally, a very generous price for the property,' he added, cocking one eye at her in an untypical grin.

'They did *what?*' Natalie exploded indignantly. 'How could you let them do that, take away your birthright and flood it with water?'

'I didn't have a lot of choice,' he said wryly, and turned on to his side facing her, supporting his head with one work-roughened hand as he looked at her appraisingly. 'And besides that, I'd been thinking of making a move for quite a while. It's a very remote property, and it could get lonely at times.'

'I wouldn't have thought loneliness would bother somebody like you.' Natalie wondered a little at the husky brightness in her voice, but before she had time to plumb its significance Cal was speaking again.

'Not me, particularly,' he said offhandedly, a wicked smile glinting deep in his eyes,' but most women object to seeing nobody but their husband for weeks, maybe months, on end.'

Natalie gasped. 'You mean you came up here just to find yourself a wife?'

He shrugged lazily and bit on a juice-filled stem of grass, drawing her attention to the strongly formed whiteness of his teeth. 'Why not? In the old days, they'd send for a mail order bride, sight unseen. This way, I get to look the goods over before making my selection. '

'Am I supposed to be flattered that you came up with me?' Natalie lashed out, stung.

'You've been the only contender so far,' he said

softly, shivering her skin as his fingers traced lightly across her arm. Her eyes seemed drawn hypnotically to the narrowed slits of his, and she felt a curious compulsion to do nothing, to let him ... 'I've wanted you from the first time I saw your picture in your father's office.'

'You don't choose a wife from a picture of an eighteen-year-old girl you happen to see in somebody's office,' she said unsteadily, unable to control the tremor that must make her seem vulnerable to this man who could never have known uncertainty in any area of his life.

'You do if she's the most beautiful creature you've ever seen, if she looks as innocent as your sister, but makes very different promises with her eyes and mouth. A girl who could keep a man happy for the rest of his life.'

Natalie's laugh was strangled somewhere in her throat. 'And now you know better.'

'Now I know better,' he agreed tensely. 'I found out that the girl I thought I was in love with was shallow, and ill-tempered, and so tied up with her own selfish aims that she didn't mind who got hurt in the process.'

Natalie jerked her arm away and took a deep breath of hurt even as she glared at Cal under her brows. Why should she care what judgment he had made on her character? His opinion couldn't possibly matter, but it stabbed her like a lance nonetheless.

'So why did you ask me to marry you?' she lashed from a pain she couldn't understand.

His hand closed on her arm and he pulled her unresistingly across him until the hard wall of his chest formed an implacable barrier to the rounded curves of her breasts. 'Why?' he repeated softly, his eyes pinpointing the salient points of the face poised above him. 'Because I think the right man can bring back that eighteen-year-old who had kindness as well as spirit in her eyes. All I see now is the fire that blazes for one person . . . yourself.'

'And you're that man, I suppose?' Natalie struggled impatiently to be free from him, to be her own person again as she had always been, but Cal held her effortlessly with one arm across her waist. As she struggled impotently, his other hand reached to the back of her head and set loose the thick coils of hair enclosed in a barrette. At the same time as it fell, making a shadowy curtain on either side of her face, he drew her down to where his mouth waited to take her indignantly parted lips.

'Let—me—go,' she muttered furiously, incoherently against the unyielding harshness of his shaven chin, knowing as the words gasped themselves out of her that they were useless. That she really didn't want him to let her go. It wasn't Cal she was struggling against, she realised belatedly, it was the overpowering strength of her own instinct to cling to the hard security of his body, to feel his need for her as a woman to grow into the same devouring want that stoked her inflamed senses.

Yielding to the burn of his kisses, her mouth softened and clung to the abrasive outline of his and she felt a triumphal surge of total female receptivity when Cal rose up and reversed their positions, every probing bone in his body outlined against hers.

Distantly, she heard Josh snicker some kind of

warning, saw Cal's head lift momentarily, then his swift return of attention to the warm invitation of her mouth. Josh's whimperings, the hum of insects investigating the wildflowers faded into obscurity. Cal was inspiring a need in her that was so savage in its intensity that she was oblivious to the world that continued its steady course around her. Her arms reached round the sweat dampened shoulders of his shirt, her palms moving moistly over the taut attraction of his hard muscles, fire leaping from one centre to another in the soft pliancy of her body.

'Cal . . . oh, Cal,' she muttered feverishly when his mouth left the loved swell of hers and went down, down in a hot sweep to the nestled fullness of her breasts between the laid-back vee of her shirt.

It was when she opened her eyes to the azure sky above her that she saw the shadowed outline of a man on horseback staring disbelievingly down, heard the welcoming whinnies of Josh, who recognised Murray's prize mount from the Ridgewood stables.

Murray! Oh, God, *Murray*! Her hands scrabbled frantically against the shoulders pinning her to the sweet-smelling grass, embarrassment and mortification lending strength until Cal finally pushed up and away from her, his head swivelling with lazy insolence in Murray's direction.

'This wasn't meant to be a public display,' he pointed out with lashing sarcasm. 'Was there something you wanted?'

Murray's rounded face, so immature by the standard set by a hardbitten Cal, resolved itself into a stubbornly youthful frown.

'I was on my way over to see Nat, but it's obvious

she doesn't need me now.'

'Why should she need you?' Cal looked at Natalie from the superior stance his elbow provided. 'Do you need him, darling?'

Struggling through a miasma of unreality, Natalie stared up into the mocking eyes so close to hers. Had any woman ever been faced with such a quandary? On one hand there was Murray, so handsome and so intricately woven into her past; on the other there was Cal with his hardbitten features and an unmistakable allure for her physical senses. But it was Cal, not Murray, who had offered her marriage. Murray, despite his inexplicable stance of outraged claimant, had made his choice of a life partner. As she had the privilege to do in equal measure'

'No,' she said slowly, letting her arm drift with obvious assurance round Cal's lean muscled shoulders again, 'no, I don't need him. You see, Murray,' she told him with husky certainty, 'Cal and I are going to be married.'

'You're *what*?'

Murray's incredulity was valid, she told herself; even she found it impossible to believe that in the space of an hour and a half she had gone from an importuning ghost from the past to a vibrantly responsive woman in the new present.

'You heard the lady,' Cal cut in brusquely, although there was an element of mocking disbelief in the eyes he turned on the sun-shimmered silk of Natalie's. It was as if he looked right into the deepest recesses of her mind and saw the hurt Murray had inflicted on her earlier. 'We're going to be married, does that answer any questions you might have?'

'No, it damn well doesn't!' Murray fumed, his anger diverted from Natalie to Cal's half-mocking expression. 'Nat told me less than an hour ago that she has no need to buy herself a husband, and that's what she'd be doing if she married a man like you. You don't even have a job when the new owner takes over at Blue Lake!'

A giggle of hysteria erupted from Natalie's throat. Stemming it, she drew a deep sigh instead. 'Oh, Murray,' she said, laughter still brimming up at the back of her voice, 'Cal doesn't need a job when the new owner takes over. He *is* the new owner!'

A comical series of expressions chased one another over his face, ranging from shock to downright disbelief. 'Is that what he told you?' he got out at last in a voice Natalie hardly recognised. 'How can you believe that? We've known him ever since he came to work for your father, and he's never once mentioned it to us. Why would he hide that kind of information if it's legitimate?'

Natalie's eyes followed Cal as he got to his feet and brushed grass from his jeans in an unhurried motion. Why *had* she believed him without question? Even the lawyer had been sworn to secrecy; Cal knew that, also that no one in the Valley could confirm or deny his claim. Not until the real owner turned up, by which time it could be too late . . . she might be married to Cal Hendricks by that time.

'I had my reasons,' he said now to Murray, 'and they're personal. Natalie knows what they were, and she's the only one who concerns me.'

Blinking, Natalie stared up at him. His reasons were personal—that he'd fallen in love with a picture of an eighteen-year-old girl and made up his mind to marry the older version? Hardly. It wasn't his style.

'Nat, you're not going to do a thing until I've investigated every damn bit of his background,' Murray decreed autocratically, and she got lightly to her feet, ignoring him as she went to Cal's side and linked her arm in his.

'Let's name the day,' she looked up at him sweetly, feeling his arm tense under her fingers. 'How long do you want to wait?'

A faint smile twitched at his lips. 'No longer than I have to,' he said huskily, ignoring Murray's exclamation of dissent. 'In a month from now?'

A month! That left a good four months before some stranger possibly came to claim the ranch ... disappointment welled at her throat, only to disappear when she remembered that it was a game she was playing ... a game of revenge on Murray for shattering the dreams of years. She had no intention of marrying Cal Hendricks in a month or any other time, however much he appealed to her physically.

'I've told you, Nat,' Murray warned again, 'you're not going to do anything until I know if what he says is true. And I'd bet everything I have that there's no Cal Hendricks listed on that agreement for sale.' He glowered at Cal and missed Natalie's pained expression. He was acting as if her future mattered to him, when she knew it didn't in any meaningful way. That it never had, really.

'Who gave you the right to order me around?' she demanded shrilly, her hand dropping from Cal's arm

as hot colour swept over her peach-toned skin.
'You've also told me I've never mattered to you, so
why the display of concern now?'

Murray's lips pursed to indicate anger, but it was
the expression in his eyes that concentrated her attention there. They had been blazing moments
before, yet now there was withdrawal in their brown
depths, a sheepish kind of retreat in face of her
temper. Something shook and then sank inside her.
How many times before had she seen that same
weakness in Murray's eyes? Dozens of times years
ago . . . but she hadn't put it down to weakness then.
He was gentle, kind, and he would never hurt her.

While she stared at him as if she had never seen
him before, he muttered, 'You know that's not true,
Nat, we've been fond of each other since we were
children.' Fond, she thought bleakly; that must be
the understatement of the century! 'You belong to
the Valley, and the Valley takes care of its own.
Now your father's gone——'

'Now my father's gone,' she retorted waspily,
wanting to hurt him for the gaping void that left her
insides hollow, 'I have Cal to take care of me. Who
the hell needs you, Murray Elson!'

It was the childish kind of thing she would have
thrown at him as a sixteen-year-old, and she drew a
ragged breath before spinning on her heel to walk to
where Josh had eaten his fill of the lush grass. She
looked back at neither of the two men as she swung
into the saddle and headed the horse towards home,
knowing she would scream if Cal followed her and
forced more conversation from her at that point.
Mixed like a boiling potion in her insides was a

tangled skein of turbulent emotions, and she needed peace—time—to sort them out into some kind of order.

But Cal didn't pursue her, and she reached the privacy of her room with only a perfunctory greeting to Bridget, who was already chopping vegetables for the evening meal. Shrugging off her riding boots, she threw herself into the cretonne-covered armchair near the window and stretched her cramped legs far out in front of her. Her hair felt heavy on her shoulders and she brushed it back with both hands, wondering dully what Cal had done with the clasp when he had taken it from her.

Cal! Dear Lord, what had she done? She had promised to marry him, that's what she had done, she told herself morosely. In front of a witness—Murray. How could she back down now, and let Murray think she still loved him?

The knowledge that she didn't love Murray any more came with a shock of surprise that it wasn't a shock. Just hours ago she had wanted him with all the eagerness she had ever known for him, yet now . . .

She got to her stockinged feet and padded lightly to the dresser mirror, leaning close to it and examining her face curiously. Surely there would be signs of the ravages her emotions had suffered that day, a shadow or two under her eyes, a droop at the corners of her mouth? What she saw was a skin as unflawed as ever, a mouth that still indicated it's good humour by curving up slightly at its ends. Her eyes met their reflection and marvelled at the silky sheen in their tawny depths, then went down to the unnaturally full surface of her lips. Her fingers lifted and touched lightly on their warm contours, and a strange pang went through her when she recalled Cal's forcefully demanding mouth on hers.

Her eyes went down farther, to the long smooth line of her neck and the beginning swell of her breasts, visible where her shirt parted. Cal had loved her there too, with a confidence no man had ever exercised on her before. She had never felt that need before, not even with Murray; a need to love and be loved in the most basic way there was. Oh, there had been moments when she had wanted more than Murray provided, but those feelings were like comparing a Boy Scout fire to the conflagration of a high-rise building.

Frowning, she turned away from the mirror and paced back to the chair. What did it all mean? Was she imagining now that she was in love with Cal? That wasn't possible . . . a person didn't fall out of love with one man and into love with another in the space of an hour. There was more to love than the physical arousal Cal inspired in her; there was— friendship, a need to be together for the rest of their lives, a *liking*.

Apart from that, Murray could be right in thinking that Cal was a fortune-hunter, a man who would lie to gain his own ends. Her inherited wealth would be her own, he had said. But weren't words cheap, even here in the Valley? Yet Cal, whatever faults he possessed, hadn't struck her as a glib-tongued city type; on the contrary, he appeared to weigh words before he spoke them, making them sound as genuine as . . .

She sighed impatiently, knowing that she was looking for excuses not to love Cal. If love was what she felt for him, then surely nothing else mattered? He could have the money, buy a place where they would live in married bliss together.

A dry smile tugged at her mouth. Married bliss just wasn't on the agenda between herself and a man like Cal. They were both too spirited, too opinionated, to live the life of people like—like Jan and Murray, she realised with belated surprise. She had never been the type Murray could have been happy with, and the same went in reverse. Jan was ideal for him, and she had never before acknowledged that fact. Murray, brought up in the way he had been, needed a wife like Jan who was domestic, loving, undemanding. Natalie knew she could never have filled that bill. Murray had known it, even way back when he and Natalie had been a twosome.

Her senses swam in a sea of euphoria as she sat in the chair and watched the sun creep down into the west. Had she ever loved Murray? Yes, but with the idolatry of youth that loved all he stood for— Ridgewood, the Elson standing in the community, his good looks that made him the prize of the Valley. She felt free in a way she had never known in her maturity. Free to live, free to love.

If Cal was surprised at the glittering apparition that graced the dinner table that night there was no indication of it in the hard-hewn features that greeted Natalie as she made her entrance into the kitchen.

'Well, my goodness!' Bridget gasped, her gaze transfixed on a Natalie transformed from cowgirl to sleek woman of the world in figure-defining gold polyester satin. 'The kitchen isn't the place for you tonight, darlin', with you in all your finery.' She glanced speculatively between Natalie and the hard-eyed Cal, who had showered and changed into a silk-like brown shirt and matching pants. 'Off you go now, the two of you, and I'll serve dinner to you in the dining room, like a fancy restaurant. Don't say a word now, Cal,' she brushed aside the objection he had started to make, 'it's about time this house was used in the way its builder intended! Off with you now!'

Even Cal seemed subdued by the housekeeper's ferociously delivered order, and he followed Natalie meekly enough into the living room adjoining the room where they were to dine in state if Bridget had her way.

Natalie was nervous as she walked to the closed cupboard where Doug Forman had once upon a time dispensed drinks to the many visitors to Blue Lake Ranch. The taut feeling encircling her throat was very obvious to herself as she bent to open the cupboard doors and said,

'It seems to be a celebration—what will you have to drink? There's——' she scanned the contents of the cupboard quickly, 'Scotch, vodka, rum, and some——' she reached down and picked up a bottle to decipher the handwritten label, 'homemade wine of uncertain origin.'

When she turned enquiringly from the cupboard she found Cal's eyes narrowed speculatively on her, and for a moment she thought he was about to refuse the offer of a drink. She had never seen him take anything other than the coffee Bridget dispensed freely at all meals, so perhaps he had an aversion to alcohol. But no.

'I'll have Scotch,' he stated in the taut, gravelly voice she was accustomed to, and she reached for one of the squat glasses on the upper shelf of the cupboard.

'How do you like it, straight or——?'

'On the rocks.'

'I'll get some ice from the k-kitchen,' she stammered, glad to escape from the room, her cheeks flaming, when he gave her a noncommittal 'Thanks' from the depths of a fireside armchair where he had installed himself.

What was wrong with him? Or, more to the point, what was wrong with her? She paused outside the kitchen, glass in hand, and leaned her back against the wall. He had asked her to marry him a few hours ago, and now he was regretting it. It was as simple as that. He certainly wasn't looking on tonight as a celebration, that was obvious. Even Cal, with his strong-man reticence, would have shown some overt signs of joy if he had, in fact, become engaged that day to the girl of his dreams.

Her eyes widened slightly as she stared at the opposite wall. That was it! He didn't consider them engaged at all; he must be thinking that she had said it to spike Murray's guns, that she didn't mean it.

She straightened up just as Bridget came from the kitchen on her way to the dining room.

'What's wrong, darlin'? Don't you want to be alone with Cal?'

An unexpected lump rose and filled Natalie's throat. She *did* want to be alone with Cal, this night and for ever. But how could she convince him of that? The feeling was so new to herself that she, who had made her living by the persuasive use of words, could never find the right ones for this most important occasion.

She shook her head. 'It's not important. I just felt like dressing up tonight, that's all.'

Bridget's button eyes looked at her with sage sympathy. 'Cal's not an easy man at times, I know. He has a stiffnecked pride that matches your own, but where there's a will, there's a way. You think on that, darlin'.'

Natalie watched with bright eyes as the well-padded housekeeper went on her way, then she walked slowly into the kitchen and over to the refrigerator. What did Bridget, married for such a short time, know of men's strengths and weaknesses? Maybe, she mused as she dug the square ice cubes from the container and dropped them into the glass, the elderly woman was the best judge of character. Not being involved herself, she saw more than the participants themselves did.

Cal's head was resting on the chairback, his eyes closed, when she went back to the living room. Her light steps faltered before she crossed over to the drinks cupboard, her mouth tightened into an unlovely line. So he didn't want to marry her, was regretting that he'd asked her, but the least he could have done was to stay awake long enough to tell her so!

She splashed a full measure of whisky over the ice

cubes, then poured another generous helping on top of that. He couldn't be less pleasant company drunk than he was sober!

'You don't have to get me drunk to prepare me for what you're about to tell me,' he drawled lazily, making her jump and spill drops of his drink on her wrist as she went towards him. Damn him and those hooded eyes of his! she fumed inwardly, setting down the glass on the side table beside him so violently that it spilled again.

'Oh? And what am I about to tell you?' She went back to the buffet cupboard to retrieve her own drink and stalked back to drop into the chair opposite his.

Ignoring the question, he picked up the dripping glass and took an eye-opening mouthful of the potent drink. 'And you didn't have to dress up like a city girl on the town,' his eyes brushed over the slender symmetry of her legs to the tight-fitting gold of her dress, 'to tell me that you're not about to marry me, that it was all a mistake.'

'M-mistake?'

He nodded surely, his brown eyes nut-hard as he studied her over his glass. 'Did you expect me to believe all that dewy-eyed hogwash the way Elson did?'

Natalie dropped her lashes, screening her eyes and obscuring the wild rush of relief—triumph?—that filled her expression. Cal had been thinking the very same thing of her as she had believed about him— that he regretted making that all-important proposal.

'Why not?' she voiced huskily. 'It was true. I—I *do* want you marry you, Cal. I mean it.' Even to herself the words sounded stilted, uncertain, and she knew that they sounded that way to Cal, too. But how could she have done better? She'd never had to find words to prove her sincerity to a man before. Always they had been the pursuers, herself the pursued. Come to think of it, her thoughts ran wildly on, no man had ever asked her to marry him before, not even the Murray she had thought she loved. She looked up and found Cal's eyes trained mockingly on hers.

'I'm sure you meant it at the time,' he said levelly, 'but there was a reason for that, wasn't there? You'd been to see Elson and he'd turned you down—that's why you were crying to the sun, wasn't it? Who said chivalry was dead in the Valley?' he jeered, his hand seeming uncontrolled in a way unusual to him as he lifted his glass and drank half of its remaining contents before setting it down violently beside him. 'Elson finally remembered the wife who married him in good faith believing that he was over you.' He gave an angry shrug. 'Maybe he is, but you sure as hell haven't got over him.'

'I have!' she cried, and found herself on her feet looking down at him, unaware for the moment that she, Natalie Forman, was pleading with a man for his love. 'I—I'm over Murray too, Cal. In fact, I—I've been wondering if I ever was in love with him. I feel so—differently about you, it's like—night and day.'

Irony ringed his voice when he said, 'So you've shucked off the old and tried the new on for size? Credit me with some intelligence, Natalie. A woman doesn't change that much in the space of a day.' He rose to stand facing her, a muscle in his jaw betraying the heightened emotion in him. 'Believe me, I'd like to think so, but I also like to think I have a brain that can add up two and two and come up with four. Tell me,' his voice dropped to a deep note as his fingers came up to caress lightly along her cheekbone, 'didn't you think to yourself after you left Elson and me this afternoon that there was no way you could back down from your agreement to marry me without letting Elson know that you were still in love with him?'

Natalie's eyes would have betrayed her anyway without her instinctively honest, 'Yes! Yes, I did think that, but later when I'd had time to think——'

'Think about what? How you could get even with him by marrying me and staying in the Valley to torment him?' The sarcasm faded from his voice, to be replaced by a note that was almost agonised when he went on, 'He's still crazy about you, whatever he told you this morning, and I've no intention of spending the rest of my life wondering what my wife's up to every time my back's turned. Make your choice here and now, Natalie,' he gritted between his teeth, seeming oblivious to her grimace of pain as his fingers dug into the soft cloth covering her arms, 'or so help me I'll make sure that neither of you wants to live to tell the tale!'

Natalie stood on tiptoe and ran her arms up round his neck, her eyes an excited shine as her hands clasped in the thick lower layers of his hair. 'I do believe you're jealous, Cal Hendricks,' she said breathlessly, and felt his left arm slide down the smooth silk of her dress and pull her roughly to him.

'You'd better get used to it,' he said tersely, 'if you marry me. I won't share you with any other man, even if he's just in your mind.'

'Nobody's in my mind.' She pushed her fingers up into his scalp and exerted pressure on his stiffly held head. 'If you kiss me now, you'll find out for yourself.'

Still he stood with his rock-like composure, his eyes assessing as they went over the eager expectancy in the face she lifted willingly to his. Murray had never been farther from her life as she pressed her hips to the hard line of his and let her eyes go lazily over his stern features one by one; eyes that were wide open now to reveal the kindling flame of swift burning emotion, a nose that was strong and powerful if not exactly straight, a jaw with no visible sign of weakness. Her eyes rested last on the firm etching of his lips and a need that was overpowering swept like a wave over her, weakening her knees and conversely lending strength to her hands behind his head.

'Kiss me, Cal,' she breathed, 'please kiss me.'

His head lowered in a blur as, with a muttered imprecation, he bent his mouth to hers and dispensed with the gentle probing most men she knew used as a preliminary. Cal's passion was instant, wildly exciting, maybe even a little frightening. But fear was forgotten when his lips parted hers and she felt the wide compass of his hands at her hips, straining her to him. She kissed him back, more and more fiercely as primitive heat burned along her veins and erupted in a passion that shocked her drugged senses.

Her hands lowered to the hard outline of his

shoulders and clung there, glorying in the sheer physical strength of him. She felt his mouth lift from hers, but only to draw a deep, shuddering breath before capturing it again and forcing her head back so far that his hand lifted impatiently from her hip to support her nape.

'Dinner's ready whenever you are,' Bridget announced from the doorway before giving a startled exclamation in an embarrassed gasp. 'Oh my, I'm— sorry. I didn't know——'

'It's all right, Bridget,' Cal told her with justifiable huskiness as he lifted his head and turned to look at the flushed housekeeper, his arms still firm around Natalie. 'Natalie and I were just sealing our bargain.'

'B-bargain?'

'Yes.' His eyes swivelled back to Natalie's, searing hers with a burning glow. 'Natalie and I are going to be married, Bridget, as soon as we can make it.'

'I hope so, after what I've just seen!' the older woman retorted tartly, but there was satisfaction behind the beaming smile she extended to both of them when she bustled forward to shake Cal's hand and kiss Natalie. She gave the latter a playful poke in the middle after releasing her from a suffocating bear-hug, her eyes blinking furiously against the tears brightening her eyes. 'About time you found yourself a real man and settled down, missy. The first time I saw him I knew he was the right kind for you.'

Natalie laughed, her hand reaching for Cal's arm, which had dropped from her, as if to reassure herself that he was there for her ... strong, unbelievably sexy, invulnerable. 'So why didn't you send me a telegram?' she teased, her voice lightly husky.

'You'd never have listened to me, just as you never did when you were a child,' Bridget sniffed without rancour, then drew herself up collectedly. 'This calls for a celebration, but I'm afraid we've no champagne, so that white wine that's been in the cellar for years will have to do. Come now to the table and I'll get it.'

She left the room at a half run and the two by the fireplace stirred to follow her. At the arched doorway, Cal pulled Natalie to him in a possessive and slightly menacing gesture. His mouth warmed hers briefly, then he lifted his head to look hardily down at her upturned face.

'Don't make any mistake, Natalie,' he said softly. 'I've looked forward to this time since I was old enough to know that there are women you want to marry and those you don't.' His hand rose to caress lightly the slender contour of her neck. 'I think I'd kill the man who tried to come between us now.'

She shook her head, her eyes a golden sheen as they met the storm-filled brown of his. 'There's no other man, Cal. There never will be.'

CHAPTER EIGHT

THE turf was springy under Josh's hoofs as Natalie spurred him on and gained the higher ground that gave a panoramic view of the Valley. The compact town nestled between hills at its far end gave way to the rolling prairie land and intermittent stands of jackpine that led inexorably to the smudge of blue Coast Mountains in the distance. To her right lay the extensive Corbin property with its neatly arranged pastures forming a checkerboard of brown earth and green pastures. On her left, Ridgewood dominated the pastoral views with its ornate façade that somehow seemed out of place in this hardworking rural area.

'All right, boy,' she reassured the restless horse as she slid from his back and threw the reins over his saddle, 'you can have a few minutes.'

She stretched stiffly and looked up again at Ridgewood's outline atop the steeper rise, shading her eyes with her hand as a substitute for the hat she should have worn. Strange that it was only now in her maturity that she could look at Ridgewood and feel it was out of place. Maybe it was because Murray was now out of place in her life. Murray who had filled her life with the fluff of dreams until Cal entered it. Although it was only days since he had formally announced their wedding plans to a delighted Bridget, Natalie felt an age had gone by.

An age when she cast off the ties that bound her to
an impossible past, an age when she had learned to
accept the love of a man like Cal in the mature way
a woman loves a man.

She dropped to the sparsely grassed ground and
hugged her knees as she contemplated Ridgewood.
How differently she felt now! Comparing her feelings
for Cal with the ones she had held without discretion
for Murray was like comparing a bicycle rider to a
seasoned stunt man. He filled every corner of her
life, and she was totally, completely in love with him.

Not that there hadn't been spats between them
even in the few days since their engagement, she
reflected wryly, glancing up at Ridgewood again and
seeing the slanting glint of sun on upper window
panes. Cal couldn't believe that Murray was no
longer a part of her life, a major part. That much
had been obvious from his tight-lipped reaction to
Murray's call the evening before.

The same kind of disapproval had marked Bridget's
plump features when she had come back to the
dinner table after answering the hall telephone.

'It's Murray,' she had tossed off with sniffing disdain. 'He wants to talk to you.'

Natalie had frowned swiftly before looking at Cal
with his thunderous brow. 'What does he want?' she
asked the disgruntled Bridget, who had reseated
herself morosely at the table.

'I've no idea,' she bit off shortly. 'All I know is
that he wants to speak to you personally.'

'It must be about Jan's birthday party.' Natalie
rose unhurriedly and glanced at the two dour faces
before walking to the door. Really, she muttered

inaudibly to herself as she went confidently to the phone, anyone would think Murray was some kind of sorcerer who had mesmeric powers over her. Her hand reached for the receiver Bridget had cast down on the round hall table. That might have been true a month, even two weeks before. Now, Cal was the shining star in her galaxy.

'Hi, Murray,' she said briskly into the mouthpiece. 'We're just eating dinner, so if you can make it short I'd appreciate it.'

There was a pause at the other end of the line, then Murray said slowly, 'That's the first time you've ever said anything like that to me.'

'Like what?' Her fingers wound themselves into the coil of the telephone cable.

'Like you can't really spare the time to talk to me.'

'If you want the truth, Murry, I can't. Bridget's fuming already because my dinner's cooling on the table. Why don't you . . .

'Nat, I have to talk to you,' his voice said urgently into her ear.

'All right,' she agreed, abstractedly noting that the pulse which would have gone haywire two weeks ago was now beating a slow regular rhythm at her wrist. 'If it's important——'

'Believe me, it's important,' he said with a low-toned clarity that alerted her senses to receive his further mildly excited statement. 'I can't talk about it over the phone, Nat, but it concerns Cal. He's not what you think he is.'

The veiled insinuation that Cal was other than a hardworking ranch man tickled Natalie's funny bone and there was a trace of amusement in her, 'Really? Do tell, Murray. I've always wanted to meet an undercover agent for the F.B.I.!'

'It's not funny,' he came back with chilling disapproval. 'Cal isn't what you think he is.'

'So tell me,' she retorted, irritation sharpening her voice. 'What kind of a monster is he?'

'I can't tell you over the phone,' he repeated conspiratorially, 'meet me somewhere. I wanted to tell you first, so I haven't mentioned it to Jan.'

'Jan's back?'

'Yesterday.'

Natalie turned and saw Cal lounging in the kitchen doorway, his eyes stony as they met the apologetic grimace she threw him.

'Oh. How is your mother?' she asked belatedly.

Now Murray showed impatience. 'She's fine,' he bit off, then went on in a softer tone, 'Nat, I really do have to see you. Where can we meet?'

'At Jan's birthday party?' she suggested tongue in cheek, not at all sure that Murray now had it in mind to ask her.

'That's another thing,' he grumbled, 'I thought you were going to set the whole thing up?'

'I'm sure you and Jean can manage just beautifully,' she returned sweetly, then with another glance at Cal's lowering expression, added hurriedly, 'Look, I really have to go, Murray, my fiancé's waiting for me. See you Thursday?'

'He won't be your fiancé after then,' Murray warned darkly, and the receiver clicked in her ear. Her hand moved slowly to replace it in its cradle. What could he possibly have found out about Cal that would make her reject him as a husband? With an almost invisible shrug, she turned and went towards Cal. Whatever Murray had found out, it couldn't affect how she felt about Cal. She loved him, and didn't that encompass trust in him too? Although, she smiled a little wistfully as she joined him in the doorway, he could do with a dose of that quality himself.

She came out of her reverie in time to see a rider emerge from the belt of trees surrounding Ridgewood and she got to her feet and pried a reluctant Josh away from the succulent tufts of grass around them. If the rider was Murray, and there was every likelihood it could be, she didn't want to face him at that moment. Not for her own sake, but for Cal's. Frowning, she headed Josh towards home.

Love and trust inhabited a two-way street, didn't they? But Cal didn't trust her, at least not where Murray was concerned. And maybe he was entitled, she reflected drily, her unbound hair bouncing on her shoulders as Josh made his unspectacular progress to Blue Lake. She had been a fool, an idiot, over Murray . . . what woman past the first flush of adolescence persisted, as she had, in clinging to outworn dreams? Thank goodness there was nothing of that sick adoration in her feelings for Cal. A wry smile touched her lips as she handed the eager Josh over to one of the young ranch hands, who gave her a dazzled look she didn't see. Her relationship with Cal promised to be stormy, if exciting. She saw him as the person he was, and she had never done that with Murray.

Life with Cal would be fraught with the complexities their volatile natures invited, but it would never be dull, static.

Every light at Ridgewood seemed to be blazing as Cal drove them up the long driveway and parked among the varied assortment of vehicles crammed into the spacious area designed for that purpose. Squeezed between a pick-up truck and a sleek Mercedes, he cut the motor and gave Natalie a sideways smile.

'Looks as if we might be stuck here for the night,' he joked with a glance at the vehicles hemming them in.

'Would that be such a terrible thing?' Natalie said throatily, leaning towards him in a deliberately provocative way. The perfume she had applied with a restrained hand drifted its floral lightness to her nostrils, where it mingled with the musk odour of Cal's cologne.

He was continually surprising her. Where she had expected to dazzle him with the deep *décolleté* of her orange flame wispy dress, he had astounded her in the living room at Blue Lake by turning from the drinks cupboard to greet her in a formal dark suit that transformed him completely into a man she felt she didn't know. The charcoal depths lent him the air of a stockbroker, although she had never seen such vibrant attraction in any of the businessmen she had known. The leathered tan of his skin contrasted like night and day with the white sparkle of his shirt, and his hair was brushed to a controlled burnish which his day-to-day grooming didn't provide. Clothes might be important to a woman's

wardrobe, but that faded to insignificance in her eyes
as they went over the jacket that needed little pad-
ding to square off Cal's shoulders, no embellishment
to enhance the lean power in his long legs.

Now, in the intimate confines of the car, she
strained towards him with undisguised longing in her
glinting eyes, wanting only to change the sombre
cast of his features to the one she was beginning to
know well. The one where his mouth relaxed its stern
lines, his eyes took on the fiery blaze that meant she
was important to the free expression of the passion
that smouldered deep under his enigmatic surface.

'This isn't the time, or the place,' he murmured,
yet his hands seemed incapable of resisting the warm
appeal of her softly tanned shoulders, the full curve
of her breasts under the flimsy covering of gauze
polyester. His thumbs flicked arousal in her taut
nipples as he pulled her with sudden roughness to
him and sought hungrily for her lips.

Natalie lay quiescent in his arms, allowing his
heated mouth free play with her own, knowing with
a sense of surprise that there was no hurry to seek
the consummation that would be the inevitable out-
come of her relationship with Cal. It was enough,
for now, that the relationship existed, and to have
the sure feeling that it would go on and on into in-
finity. There would be a time for loving, just as there
was a rhythmic time to participate in all of Nature's
aspects. Even as Cal's persistent cajolery prodded her
purring senses into a vital return of the kisses that
sent fire leaping from vein to vein Natalie mocked
her own fancy. A nature as impatient as hers could
never wait for the fulfilment she knew would be theirs

finally. But a jammed parking lot in front of
Murray's house was hardly the place for such a
momentous happening!

A giggle rose in her throat and Cal drew back to
eye her suspiciously.

'Something's funny?'

Her fingers ran down the tautened line of his
smooth shaved jaw, teasing as they traced the warm
outline of his lips. 'Even you have to admit,' she
chuckled huskily, 'that there's something juvenile
about two mature adults behaving like teenagers in
the front seat of a car!'

He grunted and set her back on her own seat. 'I
believe they favour the back seat, and I can see the
logic of that.' Easing his feet across the control
pedals, he gave her a wry look. 'You'd better slide
out this way, there isn't room that side.'

Vaguely chilled by his speedy reversal to calm control of the situation, Natalie slid across the seats under
the wheel and manoeuvred her way to ground level.

Her momentary spasm of chagrin was forgotten,
however, when she went with Cal across the forecourt to the blaze of lights and noise emanating from
Ridgewood. For the first time ever she would be
entering that magical dream house that was
Ridgewood without her girlish dream of what might
have been. Her fingers tightened on Cal's sinewy
forearm as they climbed the steps to the wide-set
porch. What she had felt for Murray, for
Ridgewood, had been as so much fluff compared
with the deep commitment she felt for Cal. Did he
know it? Surely he must.

The tawny sparkle of her eyes lifted to his and her

feet faltered on the last but one step. Was it possible Cal looked back at her with the uncertainty a young man might have displayed when he had miraculously found himself with the most popular girl in their group? No, it couldn't be. He just had that bleak look about him that would have accompanied any social foray. Cal wasn't the man to take enthusiastically to parties of any kind. He was a loner who didn't mind his own company for long stretches of time.

'Nat!'

From that first greeting, Natalie was caught up in the general excitement of the birthday party, detached from Cal's possessive hold as if it didn't exist. Swept away across the huge reception hall towards the living room, she glanced back and saw that Cal had lost none of his commanding presence by being left alone in the upper hall. Conscience smote her as an unfamiliar protective instinct thrust its way up inside her, and she managed to detach herself from the bodies that had clustered round her and fought her way back across the hall between faces she had known all her life.

At the foot of the shallow staircase leading to the upper hall she stopped abruptly. Nina Fourchette was already leading Cal away, her arm tucked confidently into his, her dark eyes glinting laughter as she looked up into his face. Acid spilled into Natalie's throat and her heart pounded in an unnatural rhythm as she turned back into the main throng. How dared Nina step so boldly in to take possession of a man she regarded as hers? And how dared Cal go with her so casually, so—so . . .

Finding haven in a wood-panelled wall niche, Natalie drew one deep breath after another to combat the sickness that made her limbs weak, her hands clench until her nails dug into the soft flesh of her palms. She was jealous, more jealous than she had ever been in her life before. Her fingers itched with their desire to claw deep gouges on Nina's voluptuous dark features, the smooth olive skin visible above the low cut of cerise-coloured dress.

'Nat!' Jan's greeting reached her through thrumming ears, 'I didn't know you'd arrived yet!'

Jan had raised her voice to make herself heard, and Natalie grimaced as she looked round the crowded hall. 'I didn't know there were this many people in the whole district,' she returned on a half shout. 'Where have they all come from?'

Laughing excitedly, Jan took her arm and pulled her through the deafening cacophony, smiling and making casual conversation until they reached the privacy of Murray's study behind the living room. The sudden cessation of noise made Natalie's ears ring as she staggered across to the desk Murray had half-sat on that day such a short time ago when she had come to see him.

'Murray really went wild this year,' Jan said with a half apologetic look at Natalie as she went to stand close to her, the soft blue of her chiffon dress matching her eyes perfectly and giving her skin a misty glow it didn't normally possess. 'He was so excited about——' she paused, her eyes glinting shyly off Natalie's, 'well, he invited the whole Valley to my birthday party. There's a lot more people here now, Nat, than when we were young. Lots of them have

escaped from the city because they want to get back
to basics, as they call it. There's the Bells, the
Lindstroms, the . . .'

'What was Murray so excited about?' Natalie cut
in abruptly, letting the strange names slide into oblivion as Jan's earlier statement sank into consciousness.
'Don't you always throw a party for birthdays?'

'Yes, but . . .' Jan's fair skin blushed a rose pink
and she blurted impulsively, 'Oh, Nat, we're both so
excited, we can hardly believe it's true!'

'Believe what's true?' Natalie came back crisply,
faintly irritated by Jan's secretive air. The only thing
that was real to her in a personal sense at that
moment was the vision of Nina Fourchette dancing
dreamily in Cal's arms to the strains of stereo music
in the living room, which had always had its rugs
rolled back at party time for just that purpose.

'Nat, I'm—I'm pregnant!' Jan informed her in an
awed voice that told of her own disbelief in the
phenomenon. 'Murray and I are going to have a
baby!'

Still absorbed in her own problem, it took several
seconds for Natalie to absorb Jan's words. When they
did penetrate, she smiled spontaneously. The years
between rolled back out of sight, and it was as if she
and Jan were discussing the wonders of what might
happen to them in their respective futures.

'Oh, Jan,' she put a tentative hand on the other's
sleeve, her eyes reflecting a measure of Jan's awe.
'Are you sure?'

'Yes,' Jan nodded happily, her hand coming up
to cover Natalie's as she looked at her anxiously.
'You don't mind?'

'Mind? Why should I mind? It's the best news I've heard for a long time!'

'I just wondered,' Jan hesitated, her fair skin flushing in embarrassment, 'if it would bother you, knowing how—close you and Murray were once.'

'Once was a long time ago,' Natalie retorted drily, moving away to give her chaotic thoughts time to resolve themselves into a pattern. Had Murray known about the baby when he had called her to arrange a meeting away from both Blue Lake and Ridgewood? Deep in her subconscious, she acknowledged now, had been the suspicion that Murray regretted Jan's presence in his life, that wanting to see her about Cal was an excuse to tell her that he loved her still. God, what an ego she must have, she told herself with tightlipped scorn. Murray couldn't have made it plainer that it was Jan he loved, Jan he had always loved as the woman to share his life.

'Nat, I'm so sorry,' Jan apologised concernedly behind her. 'You're engaged to Cal, and here am I asking if you mind that Murray and I are having a baby!' She moved closer as Natalie turned to face her and added, 'I'm really glad you and Cal have found each other. I'd never thought of it before,' she wondered, smiling, 'but you're so right for each other. You need somebody like him, who's soft and gentle but hard enough not to——' She broke off, horrified at almost speaking her true thoughts, and Natalie gave a short laugh.

'Not to let me have my own way all the time?' she finished drily, moving restlessly from the blue orbs of Jan's concerned eyes. 'Letting me have my way is the last of Cal's concerns,' she added bitterly, biting her lip to control its trembling. 'If I had my way, he wouldn't be playing up to Nina Fourchette at this moment.'

'Nina——?' Jan stared at her blankly, then laughed with comforting reassurance. 'Oh, Nat,' she dismissed scornfully, 'you don't have to worry about Cal where Nina's concerned! She's been after him ever since he came to the Valley, you know her, but Cal's never shown more than a polite interest in her.

Polite? Yes, some casual observer might have put down his willingness to go with Nina as politeness, but Natalie wasn't a casual observer. The love she cherished for Cal was something special in her life, a total commitment that encompassed faith, loyalty, trust. And trust was the last thing she felt when her roving thoughts dwelt on Cal succumbing to Nina's voluptuous charms.

'I'm just being foolish,' she voiced her thoughts aloud, starting when the study door opened suddenly and Murray's head appeared round it.

'So this is where you are,' he addressed Jan, his eyes also taking in Natalie's drooping figure by the desk. 'That young couple—the Crofts?—want to talk to you about canning the results of their labours on that five-acre spread they've taken on. Want to talk to them about it?'

'Yes, of course.' Jan went towards him, casting an anxious eye back to Natalie. 'Coming, Nat?'

'I'll be out soon,' Natalie promised, her eyes taking in the stolen kiss Murray extracted from his wife as she went past him before she turned her back to the door and stared down at the cleared desk top. Who would have thought that she could ever witness that kind of closeness between Murray and someone not herself without feeling a thing? It was Cal she loved, Cal she desired above all men. So what was she doing skulking around here in Murray's study when she should be out there making clear to everyone, including Nina, that Cal was the man in her life, the man she had agreed to marry?

Her slippered heel ground into the thick plush of carpet as she swivelled to face the door, then a gasp sighed from her throat when she saw Murray still there, the door still held open in his broad-palmed hand.

'Oh. I thought you'd gone.'

'I told you, I wanted to talk to you.' With a deliberate hand he closed the door on the party noises coming from behind its thick wood panels. 'Jan, you've got to listen to me.'

She leaned back against the desk as, in a few short strides, he crossed the room to her. The yellow-brown of her eyes held more wonder at the state of her own feelings than what he might have to tell her. This was Murray, the man who had been woven into the fabric of her dreams for so many years, yet his darkly orientated good looks now left her cold in a way that sent nostalgic shivers down her spine. She had loved him, loved him as much as any girl who worshipped the phantasm of a reality that could never be. What she had thought of as love was a mockery of what she now felt for Cal.

'Go ahead,' she said calmly, some of the old Natalie's spirit stirring as she thought again about Cal's obvious seduction by the pursuing Nina. Cal was hers in a way Nina could never understand, in a

way Natalie herself was only beginning to understand. 'I'll give you two minutes.'

From his towering stance above her, Murray
looked down with eyes changing emotions rapidly
from apology to regret to determination.

'Nat, I don't want to make you unhappy, to spoil
what you've got going with Cal Hendricks, but——'

'But?' she injected coolly when he paused.

He ran a hand through the thickest part of his
hair. 'Look, I know you'll say it's none of my business
what you do with your life, but—hell, Nat, you must
know that we care about you, Jan and I.' His well-
shaped hands clenched into fists and he thrust them
into his pockets. 'You've agreed to marry Cal without knowing the first thing about him, and I felt it
was my duty to find out if he's who he says he is. So
I've made enquiries.'

'And?' she challenged him with her eyes.

'He didn't buy the Blue Lake property, Nat,' he
said tersely. 'He owned a ranch down south, inherited it from his father, but it was far from a paying proposition. From what I found out, he just up
and sold the stock some months back and disappeared from the area. His travels led him to the
Valley.'

Natalie's chin tilted dangerously. 'I know all about
Cal selling his property down south,' she scorned.
'They're planning a hydro-electric scheme where his
ranch was, and——'

'Oh, Nat, for God's sake be realistic! His name
isn't even on the deed of sale for Blue Lake Ranch!'
White lines edged his full-shaped mouth. 'It's a
company who's bought it—Pandora Enterprises. I

never heard of them, and I'd like to bet Cal Hendricks never did either.'

Only a slight flicker of her eyes indicated that Natalie's confidence wavered momentarily. What Murray was saying was no more than she had suspected herself at one time, that Cal was interested more in her fortune than herself. But that couldn't be . . . he loved her. No man could make love to a woman in that way unless he loved her. Couldn't he? a voice mocked far back in her head. A man as self-assured with women as Cal would know exactly which buttons to press for a desired effect.

'Nat!'

Murray's arms were around her, pressing her face to the hard outline of his chest, his hand comforting as it stroked gently across her hair.

'Forget him, Nat,' he said huskily, 'you deserve a lot better than——'

'Maybe you're thinking she deserves somebody like you,' a harsh voice broke in, and Natalie became aware of the sudden increase in the noise level because of the door's opening. Slowly, she pulled herself from Murray's arms and flicked impatiently at the tears moistening her cheeks.

Without closing the door, Cal came with his cat-like tread to stand within easy reach of them. 'Maybe you're thinking she'd be better off with whatever leavings she can get from a married man.'

'You're all wrong,' Murray straightened to face him, a pulse jumping erratically at his temple. 'Nat and I——'

'Nat and you nothing!' Cal interrupted brusquely, his eyes twin fires in his lean featured face. His hand

shot out and landed accurately on Natalie's wrist.
'You're coming with me,' he gritted, and gave her
no choice as he dragged her to the door. He turned
back there to give Murray a scathing look. 'Leave
her alone, Elson, or so help me I'll see that you never
look at another woman again!'

His fingers dug cruelly into the boned flesh of her
wrist and Natalie pulled furiously against them as he
precipitated them into the hall.

'Let me go!' she hissed, aware of the curious eyes
following their progress to the double-doored exit.

Humiliation licked at her veins as Cal marched
her inexorably on. How would she ever live this
scene down in a valley community that thrived on
gossip about its members? She never could . . . never,
never!

The night air struck cool on her flushed cheeks as
they reached the porch, but Natalie didn't feel it as
frenzied panic lent strength to her efforts to loose
herself from Cal's hold. Finally she did it, and came
to a halt on the gravelled forecourt.

'How dare you!' she choked, incensed. 'How dare
you humiliate me like that in front of my friends?'

'Humiliation is something you bring on yourself,'
he returned caustically, striding off towards the car
as if he didn't care if she followed or not, and that
was like red rag to a bull for Natalie.

The slender heels of her sandals turned more than
once as she pursued Cal to the car, but she ignored
that discomfort. More important was the blazing
fury that threatened to erupt inside her. He was an
impostor, a fortune-hunter, the worst kind of man
there was!

Cal made no effort to play the gentleman by opening the door for her, and her fingers fumbled for the button clasp which refused to release until he leaned across from his seat and flicked up the button. Breathing deep to indicate her displeasure, she settled herself on the bench seat as far away as possible from his leanly powerful body. The gears clashed in her ears as he reversed out of the confined area and swept in a curve towards the tree-lined driveway.

The words bubbling to her lips strangely remained unsaid on the way back to Blue Lake. What was the use of confronting Cal with the knowledge she had just learned from Murray? He would deny it, and she had no immediate means of proving otherwise. Her body seemed one large ache as Cal drove silently home. She didn't want him to be someone she couldn't admire, respect; yet if what Murray said was right she would be a fool to accept Cal at face value.

Her hand dropped away from the door handle when, parked before the shuttered house, Cal said brittly,

'We'll talk about it tomorrow,' acknowledging for the first time that a problem lay between them.

'Why not now?' Natalie addressed the darkened windscreen, for the first time in her life wanting to confront a problem straight on without putting it off until tomorrow.

'Because now,' Cal returned evenly, 'I won't be responsible for what I might do if you tell me you're still stuck on Murray Elson.'

'I wasn't going to tell you that,' she said in a

small voice, her hands twisting together on her lap. 'Murray's nothing more than a—a good friend now. He *cares* about me, Cal,' she turned earnestly to him, her eyes glinting the moon's reflection. 'He—he doesn't want me to be hurt.'

'Then why the hell doesn't he leave you alone?' he questioned savagely, his fist striking a blow on the steering wheel as he turned to her, his eyes filled with suppressed rage. 'He's married to a fine woman, yet he still wants you.'

Her breath drew in sharply. 'Murray doesn't want me, Cal. He—he loves Jan, truly, the more so since she's expecting a baby.'

Cal was silent for a long space, his eyes trained on the meadow dappled with moonlight before them. At last he sighed and turned to look at Natalie.

'He knows that, yet when I came into that room he was holding you as if you were the most important person in the world to him.'

'It wasn't that,' she asserted hastily. 'I was—upset about something and—Murray was comforting me as any good friend would.'

Cal's eyes narrowed. 'You were worried about something? What, exactly?'

Abandoning caution, she deliberately avoided the hard scrutiny in his eyes as she said, 'Murray found out that—that you're not the new owner of Blue Lake. It's a company who's bought it.'

Cal was silent for so long that she ventured a tentative side glance, looking away again hurriedly when she saw the rock-hewn cast of his features. Her nerves were at screaming pitch when he finally spoke in the taut, hard voice he affected when angered.

'And naturally you believed him without coming to me and asking me about it.'

'What else do you expect?' she flashed, jerking her head round to face him fully. 'How do I know you'd be telling me the truth if you said you weren't marrying me because . . .' Her hand lifted in a sweep more eloquent than words.

'Because of your money?' he bit of harshly. His knuckles showed white on the steering wheel as he gripped it. 'I told you, I've no need for your money. Is it so damn hard for you to——' His mouth clamped into a tight line. 'You trust me enough to marry me, but not enough to accept my motives in taking you as my wife. Isn't your thinking a little twisted?'

Of course it was, she agreed silently, her eyes bright with unshed tears as she directed them away from him across the moonlit meadow. Her whole life had been twisted since the minute she arrived home to find her father dead and Cal in charge of the ranch. Cal, the man who had driven away all her girlish dreams of being a vital part of Murray's life. Cal, the man who had since filled those empty dreams with the reality of mature longings, needs.

'M-maybe we should wait before—getting married,' she stumbled over the words, knowing with a conviction that needed no words that if there was no marriage with Cal she would die . . . emotionally, if not physically.

'Until what?' Cal threw out with brutal frankness. 'Until you find out from deeds of sale and corroborating papers that I'm who I say I am? No, Natalie,' he gave an impatient shake of his head, 'you either agree to the date we've set, trusting me, or we call the whole thing off.'

'That's easy for you to say,' she parried his arrogant assumption that breaking their engagement was up to her, he would survive without her. 'From where I'm standing, all the trust is coming from me. You haven't a thing to lose, I have everything.'

'Everything meaning money, I suppose.' His voice softened to huskiness as his fingers trailed an evocative line across her cheekbone and touched lightly on the soft outlines of her mouth. 'Money's not important when two people feel the way we do about each other. Do you think I'd be half out of my mind with wanting you if money was my motive? You're the most beautiful woman I could ever hope to meet, but it's not just that. I love everything about you, your wild spirit that translates into the sexiest wife a man could ever have, the morals that were fed to you here in the Valley, a nature that would never make dullness part of a man's life.'

Mesmerized by the husky words of love that were all and more than she could expect from the ranchman he was, Natalie succumbed to the gentle pressure of his lips on hers. As passion mounted between them, her veins sang the knowledge that Cal loved her in the same way as she loved him, and doubts fled as she wound her arms round his oak-strong neck and clung to the hard fibre of his long form.

CHAPTER NINE

THE house was still silent and the sun a mere suggestion over the eastern hills three weeks later when
Natalie saddled Josh and led him up to the rocky
ridge where she could best view the beginning of this
new day. A special day. The day of her marriage to
Cal.

No more special day had ever existed, she told
herself tremulously as Josh, his hoofs chinking on the
grey rocks leading to the vantage point, plodded
solidly under her. Every bride from time immemorial
must have felt this sense of awe, of commitment that
now filled her, she reflected meditatively as she dis-
mounted and gave the foraging Josh his freedom. A
bridal day had that special quality, a time to re-
minisce about the past, a time to contemplate the
future.

It wasn't hard to visualise her future with Cal, she
told herself as she sat on a reasonably flat rock edge
that would provide a view of one of nature's most
fantastic spectacles. The love they bore for each other
would spread outwards like a stone thrown into a
calm pool. There would be children of their love,
strong boys and girls who might or might not want
to follow their father's footsteps into the land of ranching. Straight-limbed boys and spirited girls who
would share the heritage Doug Forman had handed
down to them.

A frown etched its way into her smooth forehead as she lifted her head and watched the first fingers of daw pink rising over the distant hills. Her father had liked Cal, trusted him with the running of his prosperous ranch.

How many times had she reminded herself of that fact in the past few weeks leading to this day? Doug Forman had been an astute judge of character, especially when it concerned his beloved ranch. The possibility of his misjudging Cal was so remote as to be non-existent. So why did she still feel this residue of doubt about the man she would be marrying later today? The doubts she had hidden from Cal with an expertise that seemed born of her deep need of him. She loved him—loved him more than life itself—but still the doubts rankled deep inside her.

Why, if he loved her as he said he did, couldn't Cal have explained the reasons why he found it necessary to hide behind a company name? It would have been so simple to quiet the fears smouldering in her depths. So easy to say, 'I'm Pandora Enterprises, and I bought Blue Lake under that name because ...' Because what? According to Murray, the southern ranch operation had hardly been so successful as to warrant the forming of a company.

But Cal wouldn't explain, for the reasons he had given. Trust ... he needed that much from her to make the marriage viable between them.

The full glow of the risen sun struck dazzlingly into her eyes and she turned her head towards the Valley, seeing the plumes of smoke rising from the chimneys of ranch and cabin down its length. Six hours from now she would become Cal's wife, making the vows that would tie her to him for all her earthly life.

And it would be that, she recognised as she turned back to the glittering promise of the sun's rays as they touched on rock and dew-speckled grass. Her commitment to Cal would be total, irreversible. She would love him, care for him, bear his children. What more trust could a man want than that?

'Oh, you look beautiful, me darlin'!' Bridget enthused with a suspicion of tears in her eyes as she surveyed the calm, collected Natalie in bouffant satin white topped by a head veil of heavy lace used by her mother and brought back to sparkling white by Bridget's industrious fingers. 'How I wish your parents could see you now!'

Natalie moved with a swish of skirts to survey herself in the full-length mirror. 'Maybe they do,' she said softly, 'maybe they do.'

The housekeeper's eyes reflected her surprise at her charge's unusually philosophical thought, but then she collected herself enough to step forward and smooth a fold in the bell-like contours of the dress. 'Murray's waiting in the living room,' she announced with a tightening of lips that indicated her disapproval of that idea. 'Oh, Bridget,' Natalie sighed, her fingers adjusting the bridal wreath on the soft thickness of her tawny hair, 'who else would I have to give me away?'

Who else indeed? she reflected silently into the mirror that sent back every curve and indentation of her slender figure. Lacking her father, who could be more appropriate than Murray to give her away?

She was giving up the old life, which encompassed Murray, and making a new one with Cal. She turned from the mirror and scanned Bridget's flower-patterned dress and picture hat. 'You're all ready, why don't you get going to the church?'

Tears glazed the old housekeeper's eyes as she looked for a last time on the slim-figured girl so calmly self-assured. 'Yes, I'll go now.' She drew a deep, tremulous breath. 'Oh, darlin', you know I wish you every happiness. Cal's a good man, he'll care for you.'

'I know that,' Natalie said steadily, then she half-ran to the housekeeper's opened arms. 'I love him so much, Bridget,' she whispered shakily, 'I really do.'

Unable to do more than pat the cool satin covering Natalie's shoulders, Bridget nodded and turned to stumble out of the room. Alone, Natalie walked to the broad window overlooking the front of the house and the white fenced meadows beyond it. 'I do love him,' she whispered audibly, 'I really do.'

Every room seemed to be bursting its walls from the impact of so many bodies milling there. The whole Valley appeared to have converged on Blue Lake for the wedding of the year, and Natalie's eyes shone with a soft sheen of excitement as she looked up at Cal, standing beside her.

'Isn't it wonderful that so many people came?' she exulted. 'We'll never have this many in the house ever again.'

'That's a thought that doesn't disturb me one bit,' he growled, running a finger round the tight confinement of collar and tie and glaring balefully at the noisily chattering groups dressed in their Sunday best. However, there was a definite softening of his expression when he looked down into Natalie's eagerly lit face. 'How long does this have to go on?'

'No longer than we want it to,' she returned with husky complicity, 'although we do have to stay long enough to eat some of the food Bridget's prepared.'

'Then let's get to it.' Taking her arm, he led her towards the dining room where Bridget had surpassed herself in the array of buffet style food set out on white-covered trestle tables. Before they could reach their goal, however, they were stopped by several of the groups wanting to heap more teasing congratulations on them. Even the pillars of Valley society, the matrons who had disapproved of the wild Natalie Forman in the old days, were happy for her. Probably because, she told herself drily, she had joined their ranks of respectability by her marriage to Cal.

How little they knew! Marrying Cal had nothing to do with respectability in their sense. He was the man she wanted to spend the rest of her life with, it was as simple as that. Her eyes misted a little as they rested on his tall, tight-knit frame, his head bent to listen politely to the advice gushingly handed out to him by the plump Mamie Gerrard.

Even Murray didn't understand the depth of her feelings for Cal. His stunned admiration when she had come down into the hall to go with him to the church had changed from hand-holding to a fiercely muttered,

'I hope like hell you know what you're doing, Nat. Marriage is a lot easier to get into than out of.'

Her tremulous smile had turned to frost. 'Well, thank you, Murray, that's just what every bride wants to hear on her way to the church!'

He'd had the grace to redden under his tan, but still he went on, 'You know what I mean, Nat. You should have found out more about him before taking a serious step like this.'

'I thought you did all the investigating necessary,' she said tartly, sidestepping him to go to the opened outer door, adding when he came to join her there, 'I trust Cal, Murray. Love and trust go together, don't they?'

His jaw clamped down tight. 'Usually,' he said stiffly. 'But a girl in your position has to make twice as sure that the man she's marrying loves her, not her assets.'

Deep in her reverie, Natalie struggled back to present awareness when Cal's fingers cupped her chin and brought her face round to his hard scrutiny. The teasing comments about bridal dreaming faded away as they looked deep into each other's eyes. In Cal's there was a slow spread of comprehension as he probed uncertainty in hers. Disregarding the joking comments that they would have plenty of time to be alone later, he swept Natalie from the room through a swirl of bodies to the quietness of the bedroom corridor and into her own room.

'Why did you do that?' she asked dazedly, her fingers plucking nervously at the smooth satin of her dress. 'What's everybody going to think?'

'I'm more concerned with what you're thinking.' He moved across to the window, his broad shoulders half blocking its light as he pushed his hands into his pockets and stared out. 'You still don't trust me, do you?'

She stared at his back uncomprehendingly. 'Of course I trust you,' she said unsteadily at last. 'I just married you, didn't I?'

'One doesn't necessarily follow the other,' he said drily, turning to look speculatively at her. 'What would you say if I told you right now that I'm not the owner of Blue Lake Ranch and never hope to be?'

Sickness churned and played havoc in her stomach. Oh God, could Murray have been right after all? That Cal was nothing more than a travelling cowboy out to land the richest catch he could find? It couldn't be, it couldn't be so! How could she have fallen in love with a man as shallow as that? She moved on jerky legs to sit down on the dresser stool, her dress billowing out on the plush carpet.

Cal wasn't shallow, she thought confusedly, she could never love a man without his strength, his integrity, his . . . But he was more or less telling her that he *had* married her for reasons other than love. Hurt twisted painful coils inside her. Why couldn't he have told her? She wouldn't have loved him less, she would have loved him more because he had been honest with her. The money didn't mean anything compared with the importance of her feelings for him. Her eyes lifted to the long straight line of his legs, the sparse broad outline of his chest in the dark suit he had worn for their wedding.

'Well?' he demanded harshly.

She met the hard blaze in his eyes. 'I love you,' she said simply. 'I wish you hadn't felt the need to be less than honest with me, but—it doesn't change how I feel about you.'

At the same time as he stepped towards her and said, 'Natalie! Oh, my darling,' she heard a commotion in the passage outside her bedroom and stared up amazed when Murray, his face reddened and his eyes holding a wildly triumphant look, erupted into the room and dragged an embarrassed Henry Purdoe in after him. The lawyer looked apologetically at Natalie and then more deeply at Cal, who had frozen in his stance near Natalie.

'I'm really sorry about this, but Murray insisted I come along with him,' the round-faced lawyer said in a regretful murmur that contrasted markedly with Murray's loud,

'Never mind that! Tell her what you've admitted to me!'

Murray had had more than enough celebratory champagne, Natalie reflected as she rose to her feet and faced the new arrivals, Cal granite-faced at her side. Added to the state of his mind earlier that momentous day, it was an explosive combination.

'I told him nothing,' the lawyer addressed Cal directly. 'As you probably know, we're lawyers for the Ridgewood property. A few weeks ago,' he looked censoriously at the simmering Murray, 'Murray was in my office to transact some business, and while the files were unattended for some minutes, he looked into them and discovered that the buyer of Blue Lake Ranch was registered as a limited company. Pandora Enterprises, to be exact.'

'Didn't I tell you?' Murray crowed, his eyes scathing as they went over Cal's impassive figure.

'He married you under false pretences, Nat, just like I told you.'

'No, he didn't,' Natalie returned quietly, moving closer to slip her arm through Cal's, her eyes a golden blaze as they challenged his. 'Cal and I got married for the best reason there is, that we love each other.'

The lawyer gave Murray a look of distaste as he looked again to Cal. 'With your permission?' At Cal's faint nod, Henry went on, 'What you didn't find out from your meddling in confidential files, Murray, was that Cal Hendricks *is* Pandora Enterprises—a company with widespread holdings in this Province—and that he does, in fact, own Blue Lake Ranch in its entirety. I think, Murray,' he turned fully to the dumbstricken Murray, 'that you owe Mr Hendricks, and his wife, an apology.'

He went from the room as if glad to relieve himself of unpleasant atmosphere, leaving Murray floundering in a sea of self-imposed embarrassment.

'Nat, I—I don't know what to say. All I wanted to do was protect you, you must know that.'

Natalie moved on suddenly energised legs to put her arms around him and hug him to her briefly. 'I do know that, Murray, and you'll never know how much your concern means to me—and to Cal.' The intricate coils of her hairdo turned in the latter's direction. 'Isn't that so, darling?' she asked sweetly.

'Of course,' he gave a brief nod, but his eyes held a smoulder of passion long after Murray had left the room to a silence that was broken only by the quick sound of Natalie's breathing, the deeper cadence of his. 'Natalie—honey,' he said as he started towards her, his steps freezing on the thickly piled carpet when she rounded on him like a virago.

'How dare you?' she raved, her hands clenched rigidly at her sides. 'How dare you,' she elaborated, breathing fire, 'make an idiot out of me by pretending to have married me for Blue Lake? You're despicable, the lowest kind of man there is! You made me admit that I—that I cared about you for your own sake, and all the time you owned Blue Lake and heaven knows how many other properties! Who do you think you are, Cal Hendricks, to put me to that kind of test? What would you have done if I'd said I didn't want to be married to a man who married a woman for what she could give him materially?'

She turned, fuming, towards the bed area and was caught back by Cal's hard grip on her shoulders as he spun her round to face him.

'God help me, I'd still have wanted you for my wife,' he gritted through tight-clenched teeth. 'All right, so it wasn't a good idea to test you. I don't expect you to understand, but it was something I had to know. My experiences with women haven't been exactly smooth running,' he said bleakly. 'Most of them would have liked the jet-set kind of life I might have offered them, but not one of them wanted what I needed, and that was a fairly simple ranch-type life, the one I was used to, the one with the values I prized.' He let her go so suddenly that her knees sagged against the high-lofted mattress of her bed. Numbly, she stared after him as he paced to the window and went on talking.

'What I told you was true. I saw your picture and fell in love with you long before I ever saw you. You

were everything I'd ever hoped for in a woman—
beautiful but nothing like the women I'd known
before. And then you came,' his voice stilled in remembrance, 'and you were just as beautiful as I'd
imagined. The only problem was that you were still
in love with Murray Elson.'

'I thought I was,' she whispered the correction,
awed by the longest speech Cal had ever made to
her. 'But I soon found out how wrong I was, that
I'd never really loved Murray the man, only the
fantasy of being Mrs Murray Elson of Ridgewood.'

Whether she went to Cal or he came to her she
wasn't sure. All she was sure of at that moment was
that she needed him to hold her like this, as if he
would never let her go, his arms strong and vital
around her pressing her slenderness to his leanness.

'I suspected that, but I could never be sure,' he
said huskily at her ear. 'You don't know the agony I
went through wondering if you were making me a
poor substitute for him, that you'd marry me just to
stay in the Valley and be near him. There were times
when I wanted to kill him because he had that kind
of power over you.'

'There really wasn't any need,' she said softly, her
fingers stealing inside his opened jacket to slide over
his warm chest to where his heart beat with a deep,
irregular rhythm. 'I was the foolish one, not Murray.
He made it very clear to me that he loves Jan, that
he always knew I could never be the right one for
him.'

Cal's head lifted from where his mouth nuzzled
her neck and he looked at her quizzically. 'That's
something I can't buy. Why was he so anxious to

prove that I was a wolf in jackal's clothing? A man isn't that protective of a woman he doesn't care about.'

'A Valley man does,' she retorted, a slow smile stretching the full contours of her mouth. 'You were the stranger, the man with an unclear past, and Valley people take care of their own.'

'I'll give him the benefit of the doubt.' Cal's eyes dropped to the lush pink of her mouth and the smile that revealed her small, evenly formed teeth. 'And if you smile at me like that, I'm going to shock your precious Valley and start our honeymoon right here and now!'

'I've been shocking them for years,' Natalie slid her arms completely round him under his jacket and lifted her mouth's eager bow for his kiss. 'And by the way, it's *our* Valley now.'

ROMANCE

Variety is the spice of romance

Each month, Mills & Boon publish new romances. New stories about people falling in love. A world of variety in romance – from the best writers in the romantic world. Choose from these titles in January.

PASSAGE TO PAXOS   Anne Weale
KING KIELDER   Margaret Rome
THE GIRL FROM NOWHERE   Charlotte Lamb
WAY OF A MAN   Margery Hilton
PASSIONATE IMPOSTOR   Elizabeth Graham
THAT CAROLINA SUMMER   Janet Dailey
PERFECT PASSION   Patricia Lake
DARK SUMMER DAWN   Sara Craven
PROMISE TO PAY   Daphne Clair
MARRIAGE WITHOUT LOVE   Penny Jordan

On sale where you buy paperbacks. If you require further information or have any difficulty obtaining them, write to: Mills & Boon Reader Service, PO Box 236, Thornton Road, Croydon, Surrey CR9 3RU, England.

Mills & Boon
the rose of romance

Three great Doctor Nurse Romances to look out for this month

There are now three Doctor Nurse Romances for you
to look out for and enjoy every month.
These are the titles for January.

ROGUE REGISTRAR
by Lynne Collins

Nurse Patti Parkin had no intention of falling in love, and certainly
had no time at all for Ivor Maynard, known as the Hartlake
Heartbreaker. With his reputation, how could she be sure that at
last he was serious?

HIBISCUS HOSPITAL
by Judith Worthy

When the yacht she is sailing on makes an emergency call at the
South Sea island of Tavalei, Nurse Rennie Phillips is shattered to
find that the hospital is run by the one man she is trying to forget . . .

NURSE AT THE TOP
by Marion Collin

When Kate Austen had to give up nursing because of ill-health she
felt she was lucky to get a post as Matron in a private nursing home.
But then she fell hopelessly in love with the Director, Simon Glaurie
– who was not free to marry her.

FREE
information leaflet about the Mills & Boon Reader Service

It's very easy to subscribe to the Mills & Boon Reader Service. As a regular reader, you can enjoy a whole range of special benefits. Bargain offers. Big cash savings. Your own free Reader Service newsletter, packed with knitting patterns, recipes, competitions and exclusive book offers.

We send you the very latest titles each month, postage and packing free – no hidden extra charges. There's absolutely no commitment – you receive books for only as long as you want.

We'll gladly send you details. Simply send the coupon – or drop us a line for details about the Mills & Boon Reader Service Subscription Scheme.
Post to: Mills & Boon Reader Service, P.O. Box 236, Thornton Road, Croydon, Surrey CR9 3RU, England.
*Please note – READERS IN SOUTH AFRICA please write to: Mills & Boon Reader Service of Southern Africa, Private Bag X3010, Randburg 2125, S. Africa.

Mills & Boon

FREE
Mills & Boon
Reader Service
Catalogue

The Mills & Boon Reader Service Catalogue
lists all the romances that are currently in stock. So if
there are any titles that you cannot obtain or have
missed in the past, you can get the romances you want
DELIVERED DIRECT to your home.

The Reader Service Catalogue is free. Send for
it today and we'll send you your copy by return of post.

-- -- -- -- -- -- -- -- -- -- -- -- -- -- -- --

☐ Please send me details of the Mills & Boon Subscription
Scheme.

☐ Please send me my free copy of the Reader Service
Catalogue.

BLOCK LETTERS, PLEASE

NAME (Mrs/Miss) _____ EP2

ADDRESS _____

_____

COUNTY/COUNTRY_____ POST/ZIP CODE_____

the rose of romance

Mills & Boon

A lovely gift for Mother's Day

Mother's Day is just around the corner—on Sunday March 21st.

So now is the time to look out for the special Mills & Boon Mother's Day Gift Pack— four new Romances by four favourite authors.

The attractive Gift Pack costs no more than if you buy the four romances individually. It really is a lovely gift idea. You love Mills & Boon romances. So will your mother.

Point of No Return—*Carole Mortimer*
No Time for Love—*Kay Clifford*
Hostage to Dishonour—*Jessica Steele*
The Driftwood Beach—*Samantha Harvey*

Available in UK from February 12th £3.00

Mills & Boon
the rose of romance